LYRICS AND LOVE IN MEADOW CLIFF BAY

SOROYA MACDONALD

CHAPTER 1
I WILL SURVIVE –
GLORIA GAYNOR

All of my stuff is crammed in my Mini Clubman. I'm taking my beloved guitar, I call it 'Martin', because that's what it is, a vintage Martin. Also, my beautiful little glass ballerina, both of which belonged to my mum. Plus, anything bought for me by anyone other than my piece-of-shit of a husband.

I was happy in the beginning ... until I wasn't. I can't, for the life of me, think of the defining moment when happiness turned into such a weight on my shoulders. I felt loved and protected and full of hope at first. All young brides feel like that, right? We had some happy times, we had a laugh together and had fun, and the sex wasn't bad either, I guess. Everyone's sex life is good to begin with right? You wouldn't marry a person who was crap in bed, would you?

I've had my suspicions that Tony was cheating on me several times over the years, actually. I never really found any hard evidence though, nothing I could confront him with. It was just a feeling. Like sometimes when he came home from the office after working late, he would smell clean and fresh, like he had just showered, or a business trip that he couldn't give me any details about, claiming he was too tired to talk. I tried to talk to him once or twice about my worries and suspicions, but he just got angry and claimed I was paranoid and trying to cause a row. If I persisted, he stormed out, and this would cause me even more anxiety, wondering where he had gone and who with. So, I just stopped asking.

The final straw came last night after dinner. He was in the shower, getting ready for a night out with work-mates. I heard his phone beep from his jacket pocket. I don't know what made me take it out to look at it or where I got the nerve from, but I did. Julie: *I can't wait to see you, big man. I'm naked and ready for you.*

Fucking big man? Is she joking?

Julie? My best friend Julie? Is this really happening? I scroll back over their messages and realise two things:

1) Yes, it's my friend Julie!

2) She is no fucking friend of mine!

I'm shaking all over, and I can't swallow, my mouth has gone so dry. The shock hits me like a punch in the gut. I sit down on a kitchen chair before my legs give way. Breathe Jo, just breathe. I've never had a panic attack, but I think I'm close to one right now. I think of all the times I have moaned about him to her. All the details I have given her. You know how you do with your girlfriends? She was always so sympathetic. She even encouraged me to leave him! I thought she cared about me and wanted me to have a happy life! I feel so stupid now. She wanted me to fuck off so that she could have him, treacherous bitch. I can't stop the tears. Although I

2

know it should be Tony's betrayal that's making me feel so wretched, in actual fact, it's Julie's.

She has been such a huge part of my life, until now, of course. Probably a case of keeping your enemies closer on her part. But no, that can't be right. We talked and laughed together almost every day. We went out to paint the town red on many occasions. She even punched a bloke in the neck one night for hassling me, now that was funny.

The four of us did loads of stuff together. Nights out, nights in, even holidayed together! Julie and Pete, me and Tony.

I feel like ringing Pete and telling him what they've been up to. I haven't got the energy at the moment, though. Pete's alright, Tony would slag him off, say he's a bit of a wet blanket. But I quite liked him. Ok, so he didn't bring much to the party in terms of wit, but he's easy-going enough.

I am going to leave, but I have nowhere to go. No one to go to. The ironic thing is, I would've gone straight to Julie. Obviously not an option.

I'll just drive. I don't know where at the moment, but I'm sure I'll know when I get there. I probably sound much braver than I feel. In truth, I'm scared shitless. One thing's for sure, I'm not staying here any longer.

Alone in the house, I have one last look around to make sure I don't have to come back for anything, any time soon. I walk from room to room. I will never lie in that bed with him again. I will never have sex with him again. It has become a bit of a chore, anyway. A Friday night ritual. Nothing toe-curling about it, to be honest. I guess that's my fault as much as his. Familiarity breeds contempt. Never a truer word spoken. I really cannot understand why Julie would want to go there. I've told her enough times about his controlling behaviour and narcissistic tendencies. She'll find out first hand eventually. Once the charm wears off.

I wonder what she would say if I asked her about it. Would she say it wasn't meant to happen, it wasn't planned, and she feels terrible about it? I could go round and bang on her door. Giving her both barrels. But what would be the point? Besides, I really do not want the bitch to think I give a flying fuck!

I've left some clothes that I've never liked, the ones that Tony would insist I wore on nights out. I leave them untouched in the wardrobe and turn around to take a last look at our bedroom. I've always thought it looks like we've just moved in and haven't added the finishing touches to it yet. I suggested adding some colour with cushions and curtains, but he was having none of it. In fact, none of the rooms are decorated how I wanted and the furniture isn't to my taste. Tony goes for the minimalistic look. I'm surprised to find I don't feel anything at the thought of leaving it all behind. Everything is too clinical, especially the kitchen. More like an operating theatre than the heart of someone's home.

I sit at my patio table and remember how it was when we first moved in. It was waist high in weeds and brambles. I remember laying that lawn; I planted and nurtured every flower, herb, and bush. I painted that fence ocean blue and planted that little lemon tree. It never gave me any lemons bigger than a thumb nail though. I smile as I look at a tiny yellow bud just appearing on one of the branches. I don't know where I am going or what I'll do, but I know that if I could take this garden with me, I would.

I think back over my life. My parents had a loving marriage. I'm sure they did in private, but they never argued in front of me or my sister. Me and Tony have never had what my parents had. They laughed and danced together and sometimes we would hear music when we were in bed. Mum would play her guitar, and they would both sing old songs. Dad would twirl Mum around when she was washing up or something and she would bat him away playfully. I loved that. Me and Vicky were never starved of affection either. It was there in every kiss on our foreheads and the ruffle of our hair as we walked by. Dad would build tents for us with the dining chairs, and I remember Mum scolding him for using her clean sheets. It was all around us every day.

A sigh escapes my lips as I close the kitchen door to my garden for the last time.

Leaving my wedding ring on the kitchen table, I slam the front door on my way out. Hasta la vista, shit-head!

I would love to be a fly on the wall when he comes home to a dark, empty house with no dinner on the table. I smile as I think about how fuming he will be.

'Morning, Joanna!' Maureen from next door waves to me as I'm getting into my car. 'Where you off to so early? You going to the charity shop?' I can see her peering at my packed car.

'Sorry, can't stop, in a bit of a rush.' I wave and quickly get in before she collars me. She's a nosey old bat, and to be fair, I don't usually mind as she's about the only person round here who passes the time of day. But not today, Maureen.

I quickly back out of my drive, and as I pull away, I can see her in my rear-view mirror, watching me go.

I can't help but wonder what my mum and dad would think. I don't even know what they thought about separation or divorce. It wasn't something I ever heard them discuss. Mum would say, 'chase your dreams and be happy', so I guess if leaving makes me happy, she would approve.

I smile as I remember summers when we were kids. My parents took us on holidays to Meadow-Cliff Bay on the South Coast. Maybe it's time I paid another visit. I remember carefree days, a beautiful beach sheltered by white cliffs, a lovely little café, and the Stern Inn. The Stern was and still is, a pub and B&B. They did the best fish and chips, and I hope they still do because that is where I'm heading. After about a two-hour drive, I pull to the side of the road and google the Stern's phone number. A friendly male voice answers it and within minutes, I'm booked in.

I feel okay to be honest, but there are two major obstacles: Firstly, what if Tony tries to find me? Secondly, what am I going to do for money? I haven't worked in years, as Tony didn't want me to, well actively discouraged it, to be honest. I did have a job before we married, one that I loved. I studied botany at uni or Phytology, to be exact. I love plants, both studying and experimenting with them, but I've probably forgotten more than I can remember now. I have been married for ten years, so botany hasn't been all that prominent in my life. Well, if you don't count my garden, that is. But I think I should be okay for money for a while, as I have some left from my inheritance. It's not enough to buy a house or anything, but it'll tide me over until I can get a job.

Starting the car and pulling back out into the traffic, I turn on the radio. Hopefully, it will stop my mind from whirling. 'I Will Survive', by Gloria Gaynor is playing, so I sing along at the top of my lungs! I feel better already. Maybe not happy, but not heartbroken either. It's anger, not sadness, that fills me as I picture Julie telling Tony everything I've ever said to her about him. Oh how they must have laughed at me. It makes me feel sick and so embarrassed to think about.

When I get close to Meadow-cliff Bay, I pull over near the cliff and look down on the bay and little village. It's smaller than I remember, but it would be, as I was small when I last saw it. Everything seems bigger when you're a kid, doesn't it? It's a grey day, so the sky and sea are grey too. My heart suddenly feels heavy as I realise how completely alone I am now. How I wish I could see my mum and dad. One hug, just one hug. I lost my parents years ago, so I literally have no one. I can't count my sister. We grew apart years ago. She's married to James. They are quite well off and like to show it. She is, without exception, the most judgmental person I know. She lies firmly in the 'you made your bed, you lie in it' camp. I've tried to tell her a few times that I'm not happy in my marriage, but she can see no wrong in Tony, she thinks the sun shines out of the tosser's backside, so I gave up trying to confide in her. I told Julie instead. Good choice Jo. Tut.

What do you think about me walking out, Mum? I truly

think she would want me to be happy, and you never know, maybe I will be.

I pull into the Stern and sit in my car for a few minutes, steeling myself. I have a fleeting moment of panic. Have I made a mistake taking off like this? What the hell am I doing? Why do I feel so nervous?

Right. Get a grip. I take a few deep breaths, then a few more. Shoulders back and head held high, I go inside to check in. The pub isn't open yet, and the place seems deserted. I know someone must be here because I spoke to them on the phone not so long ago.

'Hello?' I call as I approach the bar.

'Won't be a minute, pet, just sorting a delivery.' A minute later a man comes up from the cellar, wiping his hands on his shirt.

'Hi! No problem, I'm Joanna Portsmouth. I made a reservation half an hour ago.'

'I'm Jackson Timms. He holds out a big dusty hand. I shake it and try to smile; he has such a kind face I could cry. To my horror, I do cry.

'Now, now, pet, what's all this? Sit yourself down, and I'll get you a cuppa, or would you like something stronger?'

'No tea is fine, thanks. I pick up a napkin from a pile on a nearby table to wipe my eyes. Looking around, I choose a seat near the open fireplace. There has been a fire in there recently because I can smell it. This makes me think of my dad and the real fires we would have in the winter. He would use a sheet of newspaper to get it started and draw the flames up the chimney. A royal stand back, he called it, you literally couldn't get within 5 feet of it, it was so hot. I can almost taste the toast we would make in front of that fire, dripping in best butter. I'm staring into the empty fireplace as Jackson brings two big mugs of tea and sits opposite me. I find myself telling him the whole sorry story and he *umms* and *arrs* throughout as I snot and sniffle my way through it.

Well, pet, you've made a good choice coming here. You'll not find kinder folk on the planet, give or take a couple of 'em.' He chuckles. 'I think my old lady is on her way down, so I'll introduce you.'

Turning toward the sound of footsteps, I see a pretty pregnant woman coming through the doorway. 'I wish you wouldn't call me your "old lady"!' she says as she kisses him on top of his head. 'I'm Tammy, I know, I know, Tammy Timms, bloody stupid name, should never have married him!' She winks at him and squeezes his shoulder. My eyes fill up again. For God's sake, they must think I'm deranged.

'This lass is having a bad day, aren't you, petal?' He pats my hand and stands as a few people come into the pub. There are two old men who Jackson greets as Tom and Bill. Jackson pours them a pint each without taking their order, so I'm guessing they're regulars.

'This 'ere's Jo. He gestures over to me. 'She's going to be staying with us for a while, so let's give her a proper Meadow-Cliff welcome.' What a nice way to introduce a stranger. I say hello to them and get two lovely gummy smiles and, to my horror, I fill up again.

'Come on.' Tammy takes my hand. 'Get your things, and I'll show you your room and we'll have a bit of a natter eh?'

'Lovely, thank you, you're so kind.'

'Nonsense, we girls have to stick together, don't we? Show some solidarity.'

'Absolutely.'

My room is at the top of the building, but Jackson helps me lug a couple of suitcases up the three flights of stairs, thankfully. 'Don't worry about the rest of your boxes, pet, they'll be fine in the car park. You can see it from our back windows anyway.'

I bloody hope so.

The room is so pretty and smells of lavender. The big dormer window has a view of the bay and the pretty flowered curtains and bedspread gives it a cheery, spring-time feel. I like this room, it's cosy and a stark contrast to the one I've left behind. Which is good because I might be here for a little while, as I have no idea if there is anything to rent in the village, or whether I'll be able to afford to rent here. I really wouldn't mind living in the caravan park though. Determined not to go back to Tony, I would literally be happy in a tent.

I can hear chatter rising from downstairs in the pub, which comforts rather than annoys me. I'm starving, so I go down into the pub and order a steak baguette and a pot of tea. The baguette is lovely, full of thin-cut slices of beef with mustard and a side salad. There's some flavour in it that I can't quite put my finger on, some kind of herb, I'm guessing, but whatever it is, it works. I feel a little self-conscious about sitting in a pub, eating alone. This is a first for me. I've never even walked up to a bar on my own before. I suppose I need to get used to it. However, as I look around, people are either engrossed in their own conversations or their own thoughts. No one is paying any attention to me. Good.

When I have finished, I feel at a bit of a loss, so I decide to go for a walk around the village to see what has changed in the years since I was last here. It doesn't take me long to realise nothing much has changed at all. There are several rows of houses. They are painted lovely pastel colours on the outside, blue, green, and yellow mostly, but there is the odd pink and lilac one. As I walk by a little gift shop, I peer in the window and see little white sailboats, beach huts, and all things nautical. It's charming, and I imagine it does well with the tourists. There's a middle-aged man behind the counter who notices me at the window and smiles in acknowledgment.

The beach is as lovely as I remember it, and I can't wait to see it when the sun is shining and warming my skin. It shouldn't be long, as it's the beginning of April, and I'm looking forward to the warmer weather in this beautiful place. I feel a tiny burst of optimism. I have somewhere lovely to stay with such friendly people, albeit temporary. Screw you, Tony Portsmouth. This thought makes me want to rid myself of everything to do with him. I will go back to my maiden name: Sykes. Yes, from now on, I am Joanna Sykes.

I walk along the beach, and my phone beeps, I see a text from Tony. Without opening it, I can see it says: *WHERE THE FUCK ARE YOU?* I walk to the edge of the surf and for a second or two, I think about throwing my phone into the sea. 'WANKER! You fucking piece of shit!' I shout into the air instead.

I nearly jump out of my skin as a little brown dog of an indeterminable breed jumps up the back of my legs. I turn to see the dog's owner has a smirk on her face. 'Alright?' she asks.

'Yes, fine, thank you,' I wonder if she thinks I'm a little crazy for shouting into thin air.

She looks at me and nods her head. 'Good. Dolly, come on girl.' She whistles and the little dog obediently trots after her.

I watch her walk up the beach, followed by her little furry companion, Dolly.

She glances back over her shoulder, and I feel embarrassed that she has caught me watching her.

Back in my room, I feel overcome with tiredness, so I shower and climb into bed.

I look at the text from Tony. Deciding not to reply, I turn my phone off.

The bed is warm and comfy, and I drop off as soon as my head hits the pillow.

CHAPTER 2
WHAT A DIFFERENCE A DAY MAKES – ESTHER PHILLIPS

I wake early to bird song at sunrise. It takes me a minute or two to get my bearings and remember all that happened yesterday. I ran away—no—no—I didn't run away. I left to start over. To actually try to remember who I am, what I want, and what I like. Who I was before Anthony bloody Portsmouth came along and made me forget what it was I enjoyed in life.

I had just finished uni when I met Tony. I had started a new job with a conservation society and had just lost both of my parents too. I was sad, lost, and vulnerable. He walked into a bar that I'd gone to with a friend for a few drinks to celebrate my new job. He was very handsome and very sure of himself. He was a few years older than me and when he started talking to me, I felt flattered, and I liked it. People liked Tony; he was popular. He made people laugh; he made me laugh, and I felt special.

After only six months, he asked me to marry him, and I said yes. I could see how foolish I was before the

13

confetti had blown off the Registry Office's patio. Convincing myself that he loved me, and that he knew best, I went along with it when he insisted that I give up my job so he could 'look after me'. I thought it was sweet at first. I felt protected and loved. It didn't take too long for me to realise I had no real life outside of looking after the house and Tony. How boring, eh? Well, no more! I am about to be the captain of my own ship (if you'll pardon the nautical pun).

I'm going to ask around the village this morning, hoping that a potential employer might be looking for someone just like me to work for them. I am prepared to do just about anything. I must admit, I feel a little excited. I look in the mirror and think, *Would I employ this person standing in front of me?* Yes, I think I would. I've gone for casual smart, settling on some navy trousers, a shirt, a little make-up, and freshly washed and styled hair. I must remember to make eye contact and smile. (Not smile so much that I look simple, just enough to show that I'm nice).

I try the little gift shop first. I could see myself behind that counter. I introduce myself, give him my best smile and ask the question, but it's a one-man band, and he doesn't need anyone. He took my number in case he does in the future, so that's something I suppose.

I then try the B&B. Marion, the proprietor is lovely to me but again doesn't need any staff.

Onto the general store. Mrs Pete asks me a thousand questions, and I feel really hopeful for a few minutes. Only for her to mention that she has no vacancies at the moment. I think she was just being nosey with all the questions.

I'm getting cold and a little despondent, to be honest. So, I head to the café for a hot drink. The outside of the café looks just as I remember it. Blueish purple signage that proudly states, 'Clary's Café' with the same colour horning hanging over the windows and door. As soon as I open the door, the warmth hits me, as does the lovely smell of coffee, freshly baked bread, and the sweet smell of chocolate cake. I haven't eaten since breakfast, so my mouth waters at the lovely aromas filling the air. Mmm, a cup of tea and a jam scone, that's what I'll have.

The inside of the café looks a little different to how I remember it. It's brighter and cleaner looking. The walls are a pale blue and the tables are dressed with blue gingham table cloths. The walls are covered in framed artwork of all sizes. The artist has painted lots of them from various angles of the bay. As far as I can tell, there are some painted from the clifftop. There is a sign that states, 'All artwork is for sale'. There are no prices on them though, so I'm guessing you have to inquire.

One particular painting of the bay holds my attention. It's large, with a simple wooden frame. The colours are beautiful and someone clearly painted it on a sunny day. It has such detail and is so lifelike. The artist has captured the bay perfectly. I feel like I can hear the seagulls calling to each other from the canvas (well, I can hear the seagulls calling to each other, but that's because they are outside the café).

There's a young girl behind the counter, aged 16 or 17, at a guess. As I am about to give her my order, a woman comes from the kitchen and takes over. "Take a break, Sophie." She smiles at the girl, and then it hits me, she's the one from the beach. "Hello again. What can I get ya?"

I don't know why, but I go a bit hot. "Oh, erm … tea please"

"No problem, anything else?" She smiles, and I notice a twinkle in her hazel eyes.

"Erm, no, just tea, thanks." What happened to the jam scone?

Shaking my head at my stupidity, I sit at a table in the window and look out over the bay. It is a beautiful view and is also a welcome distraction.

I had a crush on a girl at uni, but nothing much came of it. Just a couple of drunken snogs, but when I think back on it, it's with fondness. I wonder what happened to her? She wasn't unlike the woman behind the counter really, just with shorter hair and not quite as striking.

She brings my tea over and asks the customary question when you live by the sea, "You on holiday?"

"Erm, I don't know." I feel a bit silly, as she raises an eyebrow, so I continue, "I'm hoping not. I'm trying to find a job, but I'm having no luck yet, to be honest."

"Oh right, well, I've nothing here, I'm afraid, but I'll keep my eyes and ears open for you. Where are you staying?"

"I'm at the Stern, for now, temporarily, I hope." Then I hurry on to say, "Not that it isn't lovely! And Jackson and Tammy have been amazing to me, but I would like somewhere to call home, eventually." I go all hot and my face flushes. God, I bet that's attractive!

"Oh, that's good, glad to hear it," she says. "My friends call me Dicky." She holds her hand out, so I take it and say, "Joanna Sykes, my friends call me Jo, well they would, if I had any." I chuckle nervously and she says, "Well, count me in, Jo." With that, she goes back behind the counter. 'Oh my God,' I mutter under my breath.

Dicky is my polar opposite. What with her dark wavy hair, amazing hazel eyes, full lips, and dark skin, which may be natural or sun-kissed, but as it's only April, I'm guessing it's her natural colour. She also looks toned, strong, and muscly, but not too muscly, not manly at all.

Me, I'm pale, blonde, blue eyes (I've been told I have lovely eyes though), and not at all muscly. (Something I intend to do something about).

I leave the café with what I hope is a casual wave in Dicky's direction. She smiles, and it makes me flush hot again. Bloody hellfire! What is wrong with me? I'm not a lesbian or even bisexual. I like men! I can only assume my confusion is because I have had this emotional upheaval. Yes, that's what it is. Yesterday, I was an unhappily married woman with a husband, and today, I'm a raving lezza? Ridiculous.

I head back to the Stern. Perhaps Jackson or Tammy can help me plan my next move. Failing that, I'll head up the coast. Surely a bigger town centre will have some jobs going.

I order a pot of tea and a ham salad, sitting near the bar to wait for it. "Well, you look like you've lost a fiver and found a penny." Jackson puts the tray down in front of me.

"Oh, I'm okay, thank you. I've just started job hunting around the village, and I've not been very lucky so far. I wondered if you had any ideas about where I can try next? I've been to the gift shop, the B&B, the general store, and the café."

"Well now, I wish you had asked me first, lass. I could've saved your legs; I can give you some shifts here. Some bar work and a bit of waitressing, if that'd suit you? It doesn't pay a fortune, being part time, but might help you get by for a little while."

"Really? That would be amazing. Thank you, thank you so much! Although, I've never been behind a bar in my life, so I would need some pointers."

"No problem. Start tomorrow lunchtime when it's a little quieter, if you'd like? Tammy won't half be grateful if I can spend some time with her for a change. Now the baby is nearly here, she can't work for long hours either. And I've only got Jess who works the bar, she's great, but when the weather picks up, it isn't nearly enough. So now would be a perfect time for you to come on board."

"What will Tammy be grateful for?" She's smiling and looking from me to Jackson.

"Jo is going to do some bar work for us, flower." He looks as pleased as I do. So does Tammy.

"Brilliant, that is good news, Jo! You'll be working with Jess, and I know you two will get on like a house on fire. She's taken a few days off, but she should be back tomorrow, though. So you will meet her then."

"Thank you." I can't believe my luck! I feel excited and nervous all rolled into one. I haven't worked for a long time and loads of little worries pop into my mind. What if the customers don't like me? What if I mess up on the till? What if I can't pull a decent pint?

It turns out that I worried needlessly. Jackson, true to his word, stayed by my side the whole lunchtime. The first pint I pull has a ridiculously big frothy head on it, and as I go to throw it away to start again, Jackson quickly stops me. "I hope you're not chucking good beer down the drain pet?" He then patiently teaches me how to put it right. "Tilt the glass, see? Then slowly straighten it as it fills. Look, no waste." He puts the pint on the bar. "Right, got ya, do not throw good beer away." I salute him, and he chuckles.

Jess, who has popped in to ask when she's next on shift, watches this exchange and gives me an encouraging smile and a thumbs up when I pour the next pint and get it right. Now, obviously, our meeting is brief, but she greets me like an old friend with a hug, and I warm to her instantly. She's in and out in a flash, but I get the feeling I'm going to enjoy working with her.

I try to take everything in and remember what some of the regulars' drinks are. I even manage a bit of banter with some of the old boys, which is fun, and I feel the tension in my shoulders slowly melting away.

Tom, one of the old boys, fancies himself as a bit of a twitcher and swore blind he's seen hummingbirds on the clifftop. "We don't get hummingbirds in England, Tom," I tell him. "It's the wrong climate."

"Ignore him, pet," laughs Jackson. "He's been pulling everyone's leg and going on about them hummingbirds for years. Never managed to get a photo of one though, have you, Tom?" Jackson walks into the cellar, shaking his head and chuckling.

The pub has a genuine warmth to it. It has low ceilings and red quarry tiled floors and a real fireplace (which isn't lit today, as it isn't cold enough). In the city, it's all wine bars and modern décor. But in this village, nothing is modern, and to me, it's perfect. Very quaint and charming.

The lunchtime shift is steady, which gives me plenty of opportunity to ask questions. If I'm getting on Jackson's nerves by constantly asking him to repeat himself, he doesn't show it. I love it though, and time flies by. The regulars ask me loads of questions, some of which I find difficult to answer. Mainly because I don't want to share too much about myself when it's our first time meeting. This is a new start, so I want to be a new person from who I was. Well, I want to be the real me to be exact. Whoever that is. It's been so long; my search has just begun.

Although we briefly met on my first day, I go into the kitchen to officially introduce myself to Keiron and Steph.

"Hello, I'm Jo, I just thought I'd say hi, as I'll be working and staying here for a while."

"Hiya, I'm Keiron, and this is Dracula, my scary looking sister." He points a flour-covered finger at Steph.

"Shut it you. Sorry my brother is an arsehole. I'm Steph." She gives a little wave. She's dressed in black from her black hair to her chunky boots, including dark lipstick. I assume she's a goth and would give Morticia Addams a run for her money. They are busy with the cooking, so I leave them to it. It looks and smells lovely, and I promise myself to try everything on the menu!

The following lunchtime is my first shift with Jess, which proves to be very interesting.

'So, Jo, you're new to bar work then?'

'Yes, I am, so any tips you have would be much appreciated.'

'Oh, I've got a few. Have you ever seen "Cocktail" with Tom Cruise? I've been working on this for a while now.' She picks up three bottles of fizzy orange.

'Uh-huh.' I nod, looking at the bottles she's holding.

'Watch this, I've nearly mastered it.' She starts to juggle with the bottles, and I'm quite impressed, actually, until she tosses one behind her back with her left hand, which, obviously, she's supposed to catch with her right. At that very moment, Jackson enters the bar from the cellar.

'Jessica!' He catches the wayward bottle and puts it down on the bar. 'What have I told you? You cost me £15 in broken bottles last week!'

'Sorry, Jackson, I was just showing Jo what I—'

'I don't care,' he interrupts her, 'I'll be taking the breakages out of your wages next time, okay?' He turns from her to go and winks at me with a slight shake of his head and a smile on his face.

Suitably chastised, Jess puts the remaining two bottles down. 'You might want to leave them for a bit.' She grins at me, totally unfazed by Jackson's stern words.

CHAPTER 3
HOUSE OF THE RISING SUN – THE ANIMALS

As the days turn to weeks, I start to get into a routine. A routine that I'm growing very fond of. Morning walks along the beach and sometimes in the afternoons too. I will never tire of the beach in the early mornings when hardly anyone is around. It gives me a chance to think. Despite trying not to, my thoughts sometimes turn to Tony and Julie, and I wonder what they're doing. I wonder what he would think if he could see me getting along so nicely. Bet he thought I'd be crawling back by now. I can't help but feel little pangs of anger whenever they pop into my mind. Not that I want him, I just can't believe Julie would do this to me! Do you know, she hasn't even texted me! Not once!

I quickly become a bit of a regular at Clary's in the mornings. I convinced myself it's because I love the coffee, but I am also really enjoying getting to know Dicky.

In my seventh week at the bay, (it feels much longer) I pop in and sit at my little spot near the window, when

Dicky comes over. Her opening line is, 'I might be the answer to all your prayers.' I've just taken a swig of coffee and almost spit it straight back out. I look up at her, and I'm desperately trying to think of a witty comeback, but in actual fact, I probably just look gormless.

She sees the inward struggle I'm having, so she puts me out of my misery. 'My mum's friend, Stella, has a cottage for rent! I can't believe I didn't think of it before!' She has that smirk on her face, the smirk that makes my colour rise and my heart dance. 'I don't know what the rent is, or whether it needs any work, but I could introduce you if you like?'

'That's kind of you, thanks. That would be great!'

'Stella!' she calls over to two very colourfully dressed women sitting on the other side of the café. They both stand up and come over. I, therefore, have no idea which one is Stella.

'This is Jo,' Dicky smiles. 'Jo is the one I mentioned to you, Stella, who might like to view the cottage.'

One woman holds out her hand and when I take it, she has a surprisingly firm grip. 'And this is my mother, Margot.' Dicky looks at the other woman, who holds her hand out too. I shake it. 'Hello Margot.'

'Hello, darling, we've seen you about, welcome to Meadow-Cliff Bay! You'll like it here, I'm sure.' She only bears a small resemblance to Dicky, and the difference doesn't stop there. Whereas Dicky looks to me like a jeans and tight T-shirt kinda girl, Margot is dressed far more flamboyantly in a long colourful dress, beads, big hooped earrings, more beads, and bangles that jingle whenever she moves. Stella is colourful but a little less OTT, wearing jeans and a headache-inducing, multicoloured jumper that looks a bit too big and a little bit out of shape, but suits her and, I feel, makes her look carefree.

'Are you free this afternoon to view the cottage, Jo?' Stella has a friendly smile on her face, and as I'm really keen to see it I say, 'I am after three o'clock, if that's possible?'

'Marvellous, it's number four Beach-field Lane. Do you know where it is?'

'I'll find it, no problem.' I'm getting a bit excited that I'm actually going to view what might be my new home.

I'm smiling like the Cheshire Cat, and the women go back to their table with a very jingly wave from Margot.

During my lunchtime shift, I can't hang in my skin. I'm just praying it isn't too expensive. I'm singing along to the music, and I get a sideways glance from Jackson. 'You're a right little ray of sunshine today.'

'That's because I'm going to view Stella's cottage after my shift.' I rub my hands together excitedly.

'You'll get along just fine with Stella, petal.' He has so many terms of endearment, it makes me warm inside. 'Heart of gold, she has.'

'Good because if the rent is affordable, I think I might stick around.' I smile at him, and he pats my shoulder. 'How much notice will I need to give you on my room?'

'You just tell us when you're going, pet, and that's notice enough. We'll have no problem renting it to tourists, so don't worry about that.'

'Thanks, I appreciate it.'

'You're liking it here in the bay then Jo?' Tammy

takes a glass from the shelves behind the bar and pours herself some orange juice.

'I love it, I really do.'

'Have you managed to make any friends yet?' She leans against the bar, and her tummy looks massive.

'Erm, well, I've got you, Jackson, and Jess, and I like the regulars a lot, they make me laugh, and, erm, well, Dicky is becoming a friend too.'

'Good,' she says. 'It's good that you're making friends and good that you're staying. Dicky is great. We grew up together, and we've been friends for many years. She's really lovely, you know. I wish she could find someone, though. Someone nicer than the last one, anyway.'

I want to ask Tammy so many questions about Dicky, but I don't want to seem nosey, so I just wipe the bar down to busy myself.

After my shift, I virtually run to the cottage on Beach-field Lane. It's the last one in a line of four, just before the path that takes you up onto the cliff. The exterior is painted pale blue, and I like the look of it very much. Across the road, there are shrubs and bushes, so no actual view to speak of, but at least there's parking and not far to walk to get to the beach and work.

As I go through the gate, it creaks, like it hasn't been opened for a while. The small front lawn is overgrown, with weeds all over it, but it's nothing that I can't fix easily enough. There're creepers growing over the side of the house, giving it a chocolate-box look. The front door is painted navy blue and is slightly ajar, so I knock and walk in. Stella walks through a door at the end of a short passageway. 'Perfect timing. Come in! You go and have a look around. You don't want me breathing down your neck.'

I start upstairs. There's a bathroom at the back that just needs a bit of a spruce up and a lovely bedroom at the front with a huge wrought iron bed against one of the walls, a little set of draws, and a big old wardrobe. The walls are painted white, and the bedspread and curtains are striped yellow and white. I like it very much. I wander over to look out of the window. I have the most amazing view below me. I just stand looking at it. The bay, the sea, and part of the beach are all visible. Just wow! Stella comes and stands behind me, making me jump. 'Sorry to scare you, lovely view, isn't it? If you take it on, wait until you see the sunrise. It's spectacular.'

We go downstairs and into the surprisingly large lounge. There's a big flowery settee with a matching armchair. There's a large Welsh dresser with all manner of old ornaments adorning it in the corner of the room, and a little table with a beautiful glass lamp in the centre. It all has a chintzy feel, and I love it! Nothing clinical or minimalist about it.

'I hope I haven't wasted your time, Stella; this might be a little out of my price range at the moment.'

'Nonsense, nonsense. We can come to some agreement, I'm sure. It's been standing empty for a long time. I used it for holiday lets for a while, but that's more trouble than it's worth. Just you breathe some life back into the old place, that will make me very happy, my love. Like I said, it has stood empty and unloved for far too long.' Then she generously offers, 'Keep whatever furniture you want, and if there's anything you don't want, just let me know. I'll give the drawers and dresser a clear out.'

When she tells me the monthly rent, it's very reasonable, and I agree there and then. I want to hug her, but I restrain myself. I can't believe my luck; it feels like the kind of place I could call home and be very happy in.

Stella tells me how much the bond is, which is quite a lot, but I don't care. I can manage the rent, bills, and food for now, but I need more hours or another job. There'll be no extravagance, I can tell you. But I love it enough to make sacrifices in other areas. Although what other areas, I have no idea.

As we are leaving, she points to the cottage farthest away from mine. 'That's mine, so I'm only a stone's throw away. Knock if you need a cup of sugar or anything.'

'Will do." I laugh.

'See you later then, love, and we'll sort out the paperwork. Oh, and if you could just let me have the details of your references, that would be lovely.' She walks into her cottage with a wave.

My heart sinks. Who the hell can I ask to give me a reference?

As I am walking back to the Stern, I decide to double back and speak to Stella honestly. I knock on the door to Stella's cottage, and she looks surprised to see me standing on the doorstep. 'Oh, hello, come in.'

'The thing is Stella, I haven't had an employer for over ten years, and before I worked at the Stern, I had no income. I'll find it really difficult to get any meaningful references, to be honest.'

'Okay love, let's have a think.' She moves over to the settee and gestures for me to sit.

I sit on the edge and look down at my hands. I feel myself filling with bitter disappointment.

"I could ask Jackson and Tammy? They know me quite well now. Well, they know I've been paying my rent on time, and that I'm tidy?" I look up at her and hope I don't look too desperate.

'Well, if Jackson and Tammy will vouch for you, that's good enough for me, my love.' She rubs my arm, and the relief that washes over me is visible, I'm sure.

I thought that was going to be the stumbling block that stopped me from renting the cottage. I give Stella my bank details and vice versa. I pay a month's rent and bond from the banking app on my phone, and then I sign on the dotted line. Stella hands me the keys, and I give a little squeak of excitement. We shake hands and this time, I can't restrain myself, and I hug her. She doesn't seem at all put out and hugs me back. I virtually run the ten steps back to the cottage, which I can now call my place!

I walk around the house again, flinging windows open to rid it of the musty, closed-up smell. The only rooms that need a lick of paint are the bathroom and kitchen. I'm relieved to find the kitchen has all the white goods and a little pine table and chairs, so no expense is necessary there. The back garden has a very overgrown lawn and is bordered by hedges that look as if they haven't been cut for several seasons. This does not faze me, as gardening is my passion, and I can't wait to whip it into shape.

Perfect!

CHAPTER 4
'I KISSED A GIRL –
KATY PERRY

I drive to the nearest big supermarket to buy food and every cleaning product on the market. The general store in the bay is alright if you need a few things or you have forgotten something, but it's too expensive if you've got a long list of items to buy.

I then set about making my little cottage look and smell nice. I find a little old radio in the kitchen and crank it up so that I can hear it as I work. I can't believe where the time has gone and when I take a break, I realise that I've been at it for hours. Shit, I better go and tell Jackson and Tammy that I've taken it. I got so carried away with the hot soapy water and Mr Sheen.

As I walk from the cottage to the pub, I realise this will be my short but pleasant route to work. I will never have an excuse to be late, that's for sure. Tammy and Jackson are both in the bar, and as I enter, I spread my arms wide. 'I'm taking it!' They look at each other then back at me. 'The cottage! I've taken it.'

'Fabulous! Congratulations! When do you move in?

Hold on, I'll pop the kettle on, and you can tell us all about it.' Tammy goes through to the kitchen, and I follow her.

'I'm going today, well now, if that's okay with you and Jackson?'

'Blimey, you don't let the grass grow, do you? Yes, it's fine. I'm happy for you. Have you got everything you need?'

'I have, more or less, yes. There're a few things I need, but I'll get them as I go along. Nothing major though.'

'Well, if it's anything like sheets and towels, please let me know. My cupboards are full to bursting, so you'd be doing me a favour taking some of it off my hands.'

'Thanks, Tammy, that's lovely of you.'

I collect my things from my room. It feels much longer than seven weeks that I have been staying here in this room. I feel a little twist of sadness to be leaving it. It has been my safe haven and Jackson and Tammy have helped me in so many ways. Without them, I really could not have stayed in the bay. I would still have no friends, and I wouldn't have the hope of a much brighter future that I have right now.

I go to say goodbye. 'I can't thank you enough for everything you've done for me. I don't know what I would've done without you.' I give them both a hug.

'Glad to have been of service, and we're here if you need us for anything. You are coming back to work tomorrow, aren't you?' Jackson asks.

'Of course, I am. Not only do I need this job, but I love it, really, I do.' I will need a full-time job soon though (even with the low rent), but I won't let that dampen my good mood. I can use my savings for a while, but they won't last very long. I must stop worrying and enjoy what I've achieved so far. I'll think about my job situation later.

'Thank goodness.' Tammy looks relieved, leaning over her ever-growing pregnant tummy to hug me again. 'I'll just ask Kieron to box you something up for your dinner to save you the trouble.' Before I can protest, she's disappeared into the kitchen. She can move surprisingly quickly for a heavily pregnant woman! As I return from putting some bags into my car, she's back. 'Lasagne, I hope you like it?' She hands over a large plastic box of food.

'Thank you. That's so thoughtful of you. And yes, it's one of my favourites!'

'Hold on!' Jess shouts as I'm leaving. She comes towards me with a big bag. 'Just a tiny house warming prezzie for you. I went into town to get it today." She hands me the bag. When I open it, I can't help but laugh. It's a three-foot lady garden gnome in a spotty bikini, holding a glass of wine.

'For your new garden when it's done.' She smiles, and I hug her. 'I love her, Jess. Thank you so much. She will get pride of place.'

The people of this village are so kind, completely the opposite of living in a big town. Where I lived with Shit head, hardly anyone even knew my name. They certainly wouldn't put themselves out for you or box up some lovely lasagne. There wouldn't be tea and sympathy if you embarrassed yourself by crying. There're probably some lovely people living there, but I never had the pleasure. Everyone seemed to be too busy to bother to talk to anyone else, apart from a good morning in passing. I guess if I'd had children, I would have got to know other mums. It was always something I put off, and the time never seemed right. Thank God I didn't though, or it would've tied me to him for the rest of my days. Maybe if he'd let me carry on working; I would have had some workmates. I did have a few, but we soon lost touch when I left. No point dwelling on any of that now. I am changing my life for the better; I have a job, and I'm making some friends.

The making friends part is making me feel so happy. People are actually caring and kind. This has been missing in my life for so long. Julie clearly wasn't my friend at all. She just used me to get close to my husband, then take him off me. Well, in that case, thank goodness for Julie!

I can finally empty the car of all my things, and I search for the little glass ballerina that belonged to my mum. She takes pride of place on the Welsh dresser. 'What do you think mum, lovely, isn't it?' Talking to her is a bit of a habit of mine that I can't seem to shake. I know it's silly, but I just do it without thinking. I have never, as of yet, answered for her though, which I guess is a good thing.

I'm not working at the Stern tonight, so I carry on cleaning and busying myself until I could drop. I've washed every single surface, including the windows, and gone over all the floors with an ancient hoover I found under the stairs, which smells a little dusty, but beggars can't be choosers. I sit down with a cup of tea, taking a look at my progress. What a difference a bit of spit and polish can make.

I can't wait to get started on the garden, but that'll have to wait for another day, as it's getting dark outside, and besides, I have no lawnmower or any tools. Plus, even if I had, I have absolutely no energy left.

I've just showered and put on my dressing gown (which is a little short and flimsy for this time of year) and popped my lasagne in the oven to warm, when there's a knock on the door. Thinking it must be Stella, I open it with a big smile. 'Hiya!'

'Hello,' says Dicky. 'Stella said you've accepted the tenancy, so I've dropped by to give you these as a kind of house warming.' She holds out a scented candle and a baby areca palm plant.

'Thank you, how lovely, come in,' I say, wishing I had put on something nicer when I got out of the shower. Dicky hands over a carrier bag as we walk into the kitchen. 'I didn't know whether you liked red or white wine, so I bought you one of each. Anyway, maybe I'll see you tomorrow.' She turns as if to leave.

'I like both. We could open one of these if you fancy it?'

'If you're sure, that'd be nice.' She smiles as she closes the front door behind her.

My heartbeat is beating a tattoo and suddenly my tiredness has gone and so has my appetite, so I turn off the oven.

She passes the giant gnome standing in the hallway. 'Who's your mate?' She nods towards the gnome.

'Jess.' is all I say.

'Figures.' She smirks.

I rummaged through one of the draws. 'I don't know if I have a corkscrew, but I bet there is one, there seems

33

to be everything else.' I look up to see Dicky pulling a corkscrew out of her jacket pocket.

'The girl who has everything, eh?'

'Not quite,' she replies with that twinkle in her eyes.

I try to open the red. I get the corkscrew in, put the bottle between my legs, but the bloody thing won't come out. My dressing gown falls open, revealing my boobs, as I give it some welly. Dicky chuckles. 'I have a good mind not to help you out, but I better had, give it here.' She gets the cork out with little effort. 'I obviously started it off for you.' I adjust my dressing gown. Dicky laughs, then she finds two glasses, wipes them on a tea towel, and pours two large measures. The glasses are odd; one has a stem and one doesn't. This makes me a bit twitchy, but I let it go. Tony would've chucked them up the wall if I had got odd glasses out. I am going to embrace the odd glasses.

'I'll just go and chuck some clothes on.'

'Don't bother on my account.' She looks at me with that sexy smirk.

'Go through, I won't be a sec.' I laugh nervously and run upstairs, throwing on some clean jeans and a t-shirt.

When I come down, she's in the lounge, and she says all the right things about how nice and homely it all looks. I light the candle she bought for me and put the plant on the Welsh dresser behind my glass ballerina. Perfect.

She sits on the settee and instead of taking the armchair, I sit on the settee too. We chat about the pub and some people in the village. Dicky doesn't ask too many questions, which I find refreshing.

She looks at my guitar propped in the corner. 'Do you play?'

'Erm, yes and no. I don't play in public, but I do play when I'm on my own. I used to play for my family a lot but...'.

'Will you play something for me? Anything at all.'

'Maybe another time, eh?'

'Okay, but I'll hold you to it.'

'I'm sure you will.'

My guitar holds such happy memories. Memories of my mum's patience with me till I mastered it. A time when I had buckets full of confidence. A particular favouite of mine (which I played often,) was The Beach Boys, Sloop John B.

Jolting me out of my reverie, Dicky asks, 'Hey, I tried to find you on Facebook, I guess you're not a social media fan?'

'Erm, no, not really. My ex didn't believe in social media, not for me anyway.' Dicky raises her eyebrows.

'Besides, if I'm honest, I'm not that interested in what someone has had for dinner or that their kid has managed to put their shoes on the right feet.' We both laugh.

Changing the subject, I ask, 'Dicky, what is your name? It feels weird that I don't know it.' She tuts, sighs, then says, 'It's Roberta Dickinson, but no one uses my first name, not even my mum, unless she's angry or trying to hammer a point home.' She laughs, and it's music to my ears.

'I like the name Roberta.' She gives me a doubtful look. 'No, I do, honestly.'

'Well, I've been Dicky since school, so I'd appreciate it if you didn't call me bloody Roberta.'

'Is it okay to call you Roberta if I'm annoyed or want to hammer a point home?'

And there's that smirk again. Jesus H Christ, get a grip Jo.

'Did I interrupt your supper? I could smell something cooking when I came in.'

'No, not at all. I thought I was hungry, but I'm not. It'll keep until tomorrow. It's one of Keiron's.'

'That'll be nice then. He is an excellent cook. He always puts his own stamp on every dish he makes, says it's his secret ingredient.' She chuckles. 'Never tells us what that is though.'

We drink the red, so I open the white, easily, but to be honest, probably because it's a screw top, not a cork. I notice when I take my seat that we have moved closer together on the settee. Dicky is quite tactile when she talks, and it sends little fireworks through me whenever her hand touches my hand, arm, leg, or whatever.

We finish the second bottle of wine, and she says, 'It's getting late, and you must be shattered, I better go.' I feel a wave of sadness wash over me when it hits that the night has come to an end. It feels like she just got here, but when I glance at the clock, I realise we've been talking for hours. Four, I think, or maybe five. Blimey, time really does fly when you're having fun. She gets up and goes to the front door, and I follow.

'Thanks for the presents and wine. I've had a nice time,' I say, then she turns, puts her hand on my arm, and kisses me. I think the wine has made me brave because you know what? I kiss her back. It's a bit of a shy kiss, but nevertheless, it sets me on fire. I can taste the wine, feel her soft lips, I can smell her fresh scent, and my stomach flips. I pull away and step back. Jesus Christ, what am I doing? She winks and says, 'See ya soon.' And she's gone. Holy shit, this is a complication I could do without, and I should probably run a mile from.

I sit at the kitchen table for what feels like ages, just thinking. My mind is swimming, and I don't know what to think or feel. I don't think kissing one of my female friends is a good idea, but I like her. I really like her. I think I've lost the bloody plot!

'Someone's in a good mood,' Jackson says during my next shift as I busy myself by cleaning the optics while singing Katy Perry's 'I Kissed a Girl'.

'Yes, my little cottage is lovely, perfect actually, I just need some gardening tools to sort the garden out, some plants, and a couple of tins of paint, then I'm sorted.'

'Aye, it is a smashing little cottage, and Stella will be a good landlady.'

'Yes, Stella has been lovely, so kind and understanding when I explained to her why I would find it difficult to get references.'

'Like I said when you first arrived, you'll not find kinder folk. We'll get you sorted with some tools for that garden, don't you worry about that. I bet some of the local lads will help you an' all if you need it.'

'Brilliant, but I think I'll be okay to do most of it myself once I've got some tools, but thank you.'

'Well, shout if you need help with anything, okay? I

don't want you putting your back out, I need you here, flower.'

Wilf, one of the old boys, must be in his late seventies if he's a day, comes in looking a bit annoyed.

'What's up, Wilf? You look jiggered,' Jackson asks him.

'I've had them bloody developers round again, offering even more money for the top two fields on the cliff. I told 'em, it's not for sale, never will be, told 'em to bugger off!' My eyes widen at hearing Wilf curse. He's usually such a quiet man. I've barely heard two words out of him since working here, and here he is having a rant about a farm he owns that extends across the clifftop.

'Pardon my French, Jo.'

'No worries, Wilf.' I chuckle. 'I've heard worse. What's got you so wound up?'

'Developers want to buy my land on the clifftop, told 'em no twice before, but they won't take no for an answer. They want to stick a big fancy hotel up there, they do.'

'Here you go, Wilf, get that down ya.' Jackson puts his pint of Harveys down on the bar, and Wilf downs half of it in one go. 'They can't force you to sell Wilf.'

'Aye, I know, but I made the mistake of signing most of it over to that bloody son of mine, didn't I? Some years back when I had that heart attack. The thing is, our Richard owns a substantial amount of it, and he's pushing me to sell the whole lot, including my house! You see, if we sold it, he'd get a pretty penny for his share. He's trying to use emotional blackmail, saying how it'll change our lives. He means his bloody life

38

more like, talks about me going into a retirement home! Like I'm an old man!' Jackson and I make eye contact, and he winks at me.

'You stick to your guns, my old friend'

'I will. While there's breath in my body, I'm not selling any of my fields, and that's that!'

Wilf's hand shakes as he takes a drink of his beer. He puts it down, but I can see he's still shaking. This makes me grit my teeth.

'Well Wilf,' Jackson says, 'You've got the entire village behind you, that's for sure, so don't let your Richard bully you into anything you don't want to do. None of us want a fancy hotel development, and none of us want to see the back of you either.'

After my lunchtime shift, I take a walk to Clary's. I feel nervous about seeing Dicky. I hope it doesn't feel awkward between us. I take a deep breath as I open the door to try to steady my nerves.

I wave to Stella and Margot. Margot gives me a jingly wave, and Stella asks, 'Is everything okay with the cottage love?'

'It's more than okay, Stella, I love it, thank you.'

'Alright?' Dicky nods and smiles.

'Never better.' I raise my hand.

'Good, what you having?' Her sexiness is at full tilt.

'White coffee please.' When she returns with my coffee, I'm struggling for something to say, so I ask, 'How much is that large painting of the bay?'

'I don't know, ask the artist. Mum, you've got a potential buyer who wants to know how much for your big painting?' she calls over to Margot. This surprises me. I didn't know Margot was the artist. Mind you, she looks very arty with her style, so I should've guessed, I suppose.

Margot, who is sitting on the other side of the café and is deep in conversation with an elderly lady, calls to me, 'I'll be with you in a minute, darling.' Dicky, who is wiping one of the tables down, looks over to the counter where someone is standing, waiting to pay. 'Sorry, gotta go serve my customers, see you later.'

As she passes her mum's table, I overhear Margot say, 'You two are hitting it off nicely, darling, you make a very handsome couple.'

'Don't start Mum, we're just friends.' Dicky frowns.

'Dicky, darling, I know chemistry when I see it. I grew up in the sixties, so don't you try to hoodwink me!'

Dicky looks at me and shakes her head, looking a little embarrassed. Margot isn't the quietest of speakers, so she knows that I'll have heard her.

I smile as if to say, 'Mothers!', but I feel a little disappointed that I've been plonked in the friendzone. Although, what do I expect? Could be just for her mother's benefit, *and* it was only a kiss after too much wine. And at the end of the day, what do I want it to be? An affair? An experiment? Am I lonely? I think the honest answer is yes to all three.

As the elderly lady gets up to leave, Stella calls, 'Would you like to join us, Joanna?'

I pick up my cup and take it to sit with them both.

'You are a very talented artist, Margot.' I say as I sit down.

'Thank you, darling. It's a hobby of mine. It was Dicky's idea to turn the café into a little gallery. It's been quite successful; the tourists seem to like them. Which one has taken your fancy?'

'The big one,' I say, pointing at it.

'Ah yes, good choice. I am working on a similar one at the moment. No two paintings are the same, mind you, even though I tend to paint the same scene dozens of times. There's something different in every one.'

'It would look amazing in the cottage. I loved it the minute I first saw it.'

She tells me the cost, which is a lot but more than fair, so I accept the price immediately, and we shake on it. I get the distinct impression that she has given me mates rates. I'm sure she would've asked for a lot more had a stranger enquired. I'm not going to argue though, a struggling artist she is not.

'What brings you to the bay then, Joanna?' she asks, then calls, 'Dicky, darling, could we have three more coffees please?'

I'm obviously going to be here for a while.

'Erm, well, I left my husband, and I found myself heading here because I used to holiday here with my parents when I was little. I have some happy memories of this place.' I fiddle with my empty cup.

Sophie brings three fresh coffees over and we all thank her.

'Oh, poor you, but you're going to make lots of new happy memories here, I'm sure, isn't she, Stella? You're not a lesbian then?'

I have just taken a sip of coffee, and her direct question makes me choke a little.

'Don't mind her, Joanna. She's a nosey one.' Stella chastises.

41

'Erm, not really.' I chuckle, and Margot chuckles too.

'I know exactly what you mean, darling. Back in the day, I dabbled a bit, could've gone either way, but then I met Dicky's father, Vic. That silly old bugger sealed my fate.'

'Oh no, did he die?' I say, frowning and putting my hand over my mouth. I'm always sticking my foot in it. 'Sorry, I shouldn't have asked that.'

'Goodness no, he's alive and kicking. Although, I haven't heard from him for a while. He turns up every now and then like a bad penny. He buggered off to the States when Dicky was thirteen. She was heartbroken, bless her. She hears from him from time to time, a call or a text, not much else. He went to hit the big time, or so he thought. He's a country singer, he had a one hit wonder, made a fair bit of cash from it. Then off he trots, leaving us both behind. He never really got the fame and fortune he was seeking. Hit the bottle, and God knows what else, a bit too hard. Last news I had from Dicky, he had gone back to live in Spain, doing a few turns in the pubs and clubs. Spain is where he grew up, in a very theatrical family. He'll show up when he needs something. Anyway, enough about him. What about you? Yours was an unhappy marriage too, I take it?'

'Yes, you could say that. He was having an affair with my best friend, amongst other things.' I bite my lip because I feel a bit awkward.

'Oh, poor you. You're going to be fine now. I just know it. You can always talk to us if you need a shoulder or anything. We don't have any secrets in this village, my love, and believe me, what they don't know, they'll just

42

make up.' Stella chuckles, and I laugh because I imagine this to be true.

We sit for a few minutes in silence before I ask, 'Is it alright if I paint the bathroom and kitchen? Don't worry, it won't be black or purple or anything like that. Just a fresh lick of white paint.'

'Of course! I hope you'll stay and love it as much as I did before my darling husband passed away. The two of us lived in that cottage for years and years. Most of them, happy ones.' She pauses, as if deep in thought. 'Then when he died, it just held too many memories, and I felt like I was never going to get over losing him. So, I moved to the end cottage when my tenants, at the time, moved on. It gave me a fresh perspective and helped me move on too. I miss him every day, but it doesn't cripple me anymore.' She takes a shuddering breath and says, 'You make it your home and be happy, Joanna. Any help you need, just ask. We're going to get along famously.'

Margot pats Stella's hand in a 'chin up' kind of way.

'How come you own the two end cottages Stella?'

'Oh, well, I used to own all four, but maintaining them was a lot of work, especially on my own, so I kept the end ones and sold off the middle two. It's much easier for me now.'

'I haven't seen anyone next door to me yet, do they work away or something?'

'No, unfortunately, they bought it as a holiday let, so they only pop back now and again. I'll introduce you when they come again. They usually pop in for a cuppa with me. Lovely couple.'

. . .

I feel brighter than I can remember feeling for a long time. I love this village and the people in it. It's been my lifelong dream, to live by the coast, and you can't get much closer than where I am right now! Plus, the weather is getting warmer. Lucky me.

I plan to start work on the garden at the cottage, using borrowed tools, which I still have to source. I've had a good look around the back, and I have found a small slabbed patio, which wasn't immediately obvious because of the weeds surrounding it.

I have this vision of the back garden having a lovely lush green lawn, lots of colourful plants, lights hanging between the trees, and me relaxing on the patio with a glass of something cold. I plan to make this happen very soon. I love planting and nurturing, watching things grow. Plus, gardening is good exercise, so win-win.

CHAPTER 5
TAKE IT OUTSIDE –
BRANTLEY GILBERT

I got home late from work one evening after a busy shift at the Stern. It's getting busier now, as the weather is getting warmer, and the little caravan park on the edge of the village is filling up. I'm tired, so I don't notice at first, but I'm making a hot drink and the milk is on the counter. I'm sure I put it back in the fridge before work. It's not normally something I would forget. As I enter the lounge, I notice it immediately; my little glass ballerina is lying on her side. Now I know I didn't do that!

I wonder if Stella has been to collect some of her belongings that are still lurked in the draws and has accidentally knocked her over. I check the draws, and it doesn't appear that Stella has been for her stuff. I feel rising panic and quickly go through each room checking to see if anything is out of place. Nothing appears to be, thank God. I make a mental note to ask Stella if she popped in when I next see her. I feel unsettled, but that could be due to all the drama in the Stern tonight.

Richard came in, apparently he's Wilf's son. I don't think he's very nice, as he had a bit of an argument with Jackson and seems to wear a constant scowl on his handsome face.

'Alright Richard? What can I get ya?' Jackson made a beeline to serve him.

'A whisky, and it's you I've come to see, actually, Jackson.' It's surprising how even the most handsome or pretty face can look quite ugly when the person is wearing an angry expression.

Jackson puts his whisky on the bar and straightens up to his full height.

'Oh, aye, what's up?'

'I'd appreciate it if you would keep your nose out of my business. You have no right telling my dad not to sell the land. It's ridiculous how he hangs on to it. He can't farm it anymore. He's too old, and it just sits there.' He's gone red in the face.

'Your dad was upset because the developers were badgering him again, Richard. Yes, he is an old man, so why don't you let him live out his golden years in bloody peace? There's more to life than money and a fat bank account, you know.' Jackson's voice is calm and quiet.

'Like I said, it's got nothing to do with you or anybody else in this village. I can't believe you can't see the pound signs yourself. A hotel up on that cliff will bring more customers into this sorry excuse for a business.' Richard has raised his voice now.

'Aye, well, that's as may be, but what you could never comprehend, Richard, is that we like this sorry excuse for a business just the way it is. Nobody wants or needs a big fancy hotel here, so why don't you take yourself back to the big city and your fancy business and leave us alone? Or, if you're gonna keep upsetting my customers, we can always discuss it outside.'

Wow, go Jackson!

The whole pub has gone quiet, and everyone seems to be holding their breath, waiting to see what Richard will do.

'It'll happen eventually, we both know that.' He plonks some pound coins on the bar, knocks back his drink, gives a curt nod to Jackson and leaves.

"How can someone speak like that about their own dad?" I shake my head and feel a prickle of tears behind my eyes. Poor old Wilf, he would be heartbroken if he heard his son speak like that about him.

When my parents died, I thought my heart was breaking. I cried myself to sleep for weeks and longed for one more hug, one more kiss, one more cup of tea with them. I used to tell my mum everything. I loved my dad too, of course, but I was closer to my mum. I know it's a cliché, but she really was my best friend. The hole my mum left behind is bigger than she ever was. She spent hours teaching me the guitar, all sixties and seventies music, and I loved it. Whereas, our Vicky was the daddy's girl; she followed him around like a little puppy. I really don't think I'd have married Tony if they were alive.

To think that someone could be hoping for one of their parents to die is absolutely beyond me ... Wilf is such a lovely old man. According to Jackson, he has been on that farm his whole life, as was his dad before him.

I feel so sad for Wilf. 'Do you think Wilf is lonely up there on his own, Jackson?'

He shakes his head. 'Not a chance, all the old women of the village fuss over him, taking him cakes and the like. He loves it up there, and he's loved down here too. This'll be the death of him, all this stress at his age.'

'Don't let Wilf hear you say that. He's not an old man, you know!' We both smile sadly.

The Stern is like a village hall. It's a real hub of activity a lot of the time. I love that about it. It doubles up as a playgroup/coffee morning on Wednesday mornings, and it's where everyone's business gets aired, then usually sorted, and where we hold the village parish meetings, overseen by Mrs Pete from the general store. She's a skinny, beady-eyed old woman. She doesn't miss a trick and is probably the nosiest woman alive, but she has a heart of gold and only the village's best interests in mind too.

I'm behind the bar one night, during one such meeting, and I can't help but smile at the agenda. Dog poo on the cliff path seems to be the general contention and dominates the majority of the evening. When I whisper this to Jackson, he says it's on the agenda every meeting and as of yet, no one has come up with a solution. There's talk of CCTV being set up, then dismissed as being too expensive, someone suggests undercover surveillance in which a brief argument ensues because no one actually wants to sit in a bush, waiting for a dog to shit on the path. I'm so glad Jess is in the cellar for this agenda item because she would definitely have something to say, and we would be howling with laughter. Mrs Pete loses patience, and it is decided that each villager will keep a lookout for the culprit and be armed with dog poo bags so that they can pick up any they see on the footpath.

'Okay, let's move on. I have another very serious matter to discuss.' She looks over the top of her glasses to make sure she has everyone's attention. 'Milk and other items are going missing from doorsteps when the milkman has done his delivery in the mornings. Has anyone else noticed anything missing?' She looks around the room and waits a beat. 'I've had similar things go missing from the store, like ham and cheese. This is becoming a regular occurrence. I would like to say that I think it's the tourists, but this has been happening since before the summer season started, so I'm going to be quite frank and say I suspect the culprit is young Jake O'Brien.' There's a general mumble of agreement and lots of head nodding.

'Hold on,' Jackson says from behind the bar, shaking his head. 'We can't accuse anyone of anything with nothing to go on except suspicion.'

'Well, he's been in trouble before. The bobbies have been to his house a few times. It wouldn't surprise me at all,' Bill, one of the old boys, chimes in.

'Okay, let's not jump to conclusions. That's all I'm saying. I'll have a word with his mother and him when I see them. He might be innocent. Just remember that.' This seems to pacify everyone a little, as the general hubbub dies down. If Jackson says he will look into something, then he will.

Jess whispers in my ear, 'It's probably not Jake at all. He gets the blame for everything, could just as easily be Steph.'

'What? Our Steph? Steph, who works in the kitchen?'

'Yes, the very same. She used to be light-fingered. Jackson and Tammy gave her a chance, for Keiron's sake, really. What Jackson hasn't mentioned, because he's too nice, is that he's had some meat and a bottle of vodka go missing too. If I find out she's shitting on Jackson and Tammy, I'll knock her out.'

Before I have a chance to say anything, Mrs Pete says, 'Okay everyone, we will now bring the meeting to a close. Thank you for your suggestions and for coming tonight.' As people are standing to leave, Dicky comes in. She doesn't look like herself, paler than usual. She says in a voice loud enough for everyone to hear, 'Wilf has died. Gladys took a pie up there for his dinner, and he was in his armchair. He was cold. He'd gone. Nothing anyone could do.'

A hushed silence falls over the pub. No one knows what to say. There's just genuine sadness on everyone's face. I notice a tear trickle down Dicky's face, so I go round the bar to give her a hug.

From what I know of her, she wouldn't want people to see her cry. She gently removes herself from my arms with a watery smile, wipes her cheek, and asks me to get her a brandy. 'He was like a granddad to me, you know. I've known him all my life. Mum used to look after Richard for them when he was little. They had him late in life, and I used to go up there with her. I spent many a happy day playing on the tractors and getting a bollockin' off Wilf.' She drinks her brandy down then says, 'I better go, Jo. See you tomorrow morning at the café?'

'Yeah, take care, Dicky.' Although I'm sad to see her go, I do understand completely that when you've had a shock, you might want to be on your own for a while.

'Before you all go,' Jackson calls, 'I would just like to say, in true Meadow-Cliff style, we're gonna give Wilf the best send off this village has ever seen. Come and have a drink on the house, and let us raise a glass to one of the bay's finest!' Jackson and I are busy for a while dolling out drinks to all the villagers.

There's a sad expression on each and every face, and what feels like a dark cloud in the air that, in the short while since I've been here, has not been present.

As I'm walking home to the cottage, my phone bleeps the arrival of a text. I can see it's from our Vicky:

I bumped into Tony today, Joanna. He said you've done a disappearing act and snuck off! Without telling anyone! He's out of his mind with worry. How can you be so selfish?

Delete.

The Stern is busy over the next few weeks, planning Wilf's wake. Everyone has ideas, and everyone wants to be involved. 'Won't Richard be annoyed that we've taken over the planning of his father's wake, Jackson?'

'You would think so, wouldn't you? I tried ringing and texting him, but I didn't get a reply. So, I sent an email to his company, telling him what we are doing, asking him if it's ok, and if he wanted to be part of the planning, or wanted anything in particular, but he replied that after the interment, he would be heading straight back to the city so to do as we like. So, we are. If it was left to him, old Wilf probably wouldn't even have a wake. He'd turn in his grave. Big on wakes is this village.'

'Miserable bugger,' says Jess, 'I mean, obviously, I wouldn't say no, but I've never seen him laugh, not once.'

Tammy was right. Jess and I do get on like a house on fire. We've become very good friends. No one has ever made me laugh like Jess does. I love listening to her funny, bubbly chatter behind the bar, and the customers love her cheeky banter. She says things that I would never dare to say and probably wouldn't think of. She looks just like what she is, short, curvy, pretty, and fun-loving.

'Jess! Surely you don't fancy Richard,' I whisper, looking around the bar to check no one is listening.

'Too right I bloody do! Have you seen him? Tall, dark, muscly, and handsome.' She has this moody look on her face.

'Cocky, I'd call it, Jess, and I don't want to burst your little bubble, but he doesn't come over as a very nice man, to be honest.'

'Well, I bet I could soften him up, or on second thoughts, soft is not something I want him to be. Besides, I don't think he's even noticed me despite the fact I've seen him thousands of times. I bet he likes tall leggy blondes with fake lips, tits and eyelashes.' She sighs.

This makes me laugh. Why she hasn't been snapped up, I do not know. However, she gets her fair share of casual flings. I know this because, I get a blow-by-blow account. Although, I get the feeling sometimes that she would like a proper relationship.

Old Tom is standing at the bar, oblivious to Jess'

chatter. He is looking at his phone and shaking his head.

'What's the matter, Tom?' I ask.

'One of the grandkiddies showed me how to take a photo on me new phone, but I can't find 'em now. He was up there again this morning, you know.'

'The hummingbird?'

'Yes, hovering over the flowers on the cliff, he was. I took some photos to prove to all the naysayers that he exists, but I'll be buggered if I can find them now.'

'Okay, let me have a look for you.' I hold out my hand, and he passes the phone to me.

'I hope you haven't got any dick pics on there, Tom,' laughs Jess.

'What's she saying?' He puts his hand to his ear and cups it, trying to hear her.

'Nothing,' I say, glaring at Jess, who finds the whole situation hilarious.

I scroll through his recent photos and realise why he can't find his photos of his 'hummingbird'

'They are all pictures of your eye, Tom; you've got the camera on selfie mode.'

'What? What are you on about? I took a dozen pictures this morning.' He's doing a lot of tutting and sounds frustrated.

'"Eye, eye", Captain.' Jess chuckles as she salutes him.

I ignore her and speak to Tom. 'Yes, you did, but they are all of your eye, look.' I hold out the phone so that he can see what I mean.

'I've deleted them for you and changed it now, so when you take a photo, it will be of something in front of you, look.' I hold the phone up, so he can see that he has a view of the pub, not himself.

'Well, thank you, I suppose, although why you deleted all my photos of that lovely bird, I cannot fathom,' he says, shaking his head again.

I hear Jess splutter with laughter behind me.

The next few weeks fly by, as the bar is busy with an influx of people on their summer holiday. We have also been busy preparing for Wilf's wake, so I haven't seen much of Dicky, apart from my morning coffee at Clary's. It's a beautiful day, so I go out early to walk along the beach. I savour my early morning walks before anyone is around.

The sound and smell of the ocean and the seagull's cry is the perfect way to start the day. I love looking at what the people the day before have created in the sand, too far back on the beach for the tide to have taken them. I always pick up just one shell to take back to my garden. I like trying to find a perfect one that the sea has brought in overnight.

I sit down to look at the sea and notice someone is surfing. He (or she) is very good and catches the waves with practised ease. I can see now that the surfer is a she, and I envy her skill and grace. I have had a go at surfing a few times on holidays, but I never really mastered it. I would kill to be able to ride the waves like that. How liberating and free it must feel. I had a few lessons once, and although the tutor was very experienced and encouraging, I didn't really get any further than using my surfboard as a bodyboard.

She gets out of the sea with her surfboard under her arm and starts towards me. It's Dicky. For Christ's sake, this woman just gets hotter.

'Impressive,' I say as she gets close enough to hear me.

'I thought it was you.' She shakes water from her hair and sprays my face in the process.

Dicky peels the top half of her wetsuit down, revealing a tiny red bikini top.

Eat your heart out, Baywatch babe.

'Perhaps you could give me a lesson sometime?' I ask. Although this could be embarrassing on my part, it's a great excuse to spend some time with her when neither of us is behind a counter or bar.

'Lessons in what?' She has that twinkle in her eye and is inwardly laughing at me, I'm sure.

'Erm, surfing?' I feel my colour rise and feel embarrassed that this woman is having this effect on me.

'You're on, have you got a wetsuit? The water is quite cold early in the mornings, even in the summer.'

'Ah, no, I haven't. Never mind, it was just a thought.' I am transfixed as I watch droplets work their way down her lovely tanned skin.

'You don't get out of it that easily. I have a few, they are old, but they'll do the job. Come round, and you can try one on if you're serious?'"

'Okay, great.' I think I sound a bit too eager, but what the hell. 'Although, I'm not sure what I will look like in a wetsuit.' Probably like a chubby baby seal.

'Hey, there's nothing wrong with you, Jo, nothing at all." She fixes me with her lovely eyes, and I look down at the sand.

'I've been meaning to ask, are you going to the Full Moon party at the Stern or are you working it?'

'Yes, I'll be there. I asked Jackson if he needed me, and he doesn't, so I guess I'll be on the right side of the bar tonight.'

'It happens every year, usually when there's a full moon, but that's not a given.' She laughs then adds, 'Jackson was going to cancel because we haven't laid poor Wilf to rest yet, but everyone agreed that life must go on, and he said Wilf would be mad if we cancelled on his behalf.'

'Yeah, he said the same to me.' My smile just got wider, and my heart just increased its pace. I know it's not a date or anything, but... 'I'm looking forward to it already.'

'Good, see you tonight then, don't forget to wear white!' Then she adds, 'Much as I would love to spend the day on the beach with you, I've gotta go and walk Dolly, then set up the café, so see you later.'

'Yeah, you will.' I watch her retreat up the beach, carrying her board, her skin still wet and her back toned. I just can't help but watch her. She interests me like no other female ever has.

As she goes, I'm thinking, if she turns back, she's interested in me. I play these little games in my head all the time. She's in no hurry, and she is almost off the beach. I think she isn't going to look back when she steps onto the footpath and turns, putting her hand up. I do the same. I'm suddenly not sure if this is a good thing or not. I came here to find myself again, not find a new romance or whatever. And especially not with the same sex! It's just messing with my head.

CHAPTER 6

BAD MOON RISING – CREEDENCE CLEARWATER REVIVAL

The Full Moon party preparations are in full swing. Jackson has strewn the garden with enough white lights to be seen from space. There's a hog roasting on a spit and a stage being erected at the bottom of the garden. A small army of people are working on it, and I feel so excited. I can't wait, although I feel a bit nervous. God only knows why.

What I wear and how I look are suddenly very important to me. I've always cared about my appearance, of course, but I rarely went out, and when I did, it was always with Tony, and he usually chose what I wore. Today, I'm going the whole hog: hair, face, nails, shaved ... erm, legs. I want to look nice—no more than nice—I want to look pretty. Beautiful might be a stretch, so pretty would be good.

I've borrowed one of Tammy's dresses, as I haven't brought anything suitable with me. It's white, apart from some turquoise piping, and low enough to make my boobs look nice and full. Not 'here's my boobs, I'll see you in a bit' big. But definitely 'get a load of these puppies' big. Tony hated it if I wore anything a bit revealing. So, all the more reason to wear it. I've got some flat sandals and a turquoise necklace and matching dangly earrings, courtesy of the little gift shop. Teamed with my denim jacket in case it gets chilly, I should look alright.

I spend ages getting ready: hair up, hair down, straightened, curled, hair back up in a messy bun. When I eventually stand in front of my full-length mirror, I actually like what I see. This is a new feeling to me, and what a refreshing change. I wanted to be pretty, and I think I've achieved it.

As I near the garden, I can hear music. I go round the back of the pub and through the gate. Oh wow, the garden looks beautiful, even though I was here when it was being set up. Now that it's almost dark, the lights look amazing, and the smell of the hog roast makes my mouth water. Jackson has drafted in nearly every young person in the village (not that there's that many) to glass collect and wash up.

I stand looking around for several minutes, wondering where to sit. Most of the tables have people already sitting at them, and I don't recognise anyone. Where's Dicky? I can't stand here all night feeling silly, so I turn to go into the bar when I hear someone call my name. Margot and Stella are sitting at a table near the stage, and they wave me over.

As I weave my way through the tables and get closer, I recognise quite a lot of people. Everyone looks so different dressed up. Margot has on a lovely white floaty number teamed with more jewellery than you can shake a stick at. Stella has on jeans and a mid-length white caftan, and she too has on lots of jewellery. They both look lovely.

'What would you ladies like to drink? I'll just pop to the bar,' I ask them.

'Oh, sit yourself down, Joanna, Dicky is at the bar, darling. We saw you lurking in the gateway, so she's gone to get us all one.' Margot pats the table in front of her.

As I sit, I see Dicky coming towards us with a tray of drinks. Oh my god, she looks stunning. She is wearing her dark curly hair down, which is bouncing around her shoulders as she walks. I've only ever seen her hair up in a ponytail, or wet from the sea, and it really is lovely. She has on a white dress that hugs her body in all the right places with high strappy sandals. The sight of her literally takes my breath away. Get a grip.

'Here we go, ladies.' Dicky puts the tray of drinks on the table and sits next to me. I notice, in addition to our usual drinks, there's a shot for each of us too, as well as a lemon slice each and a small salt pot. Oh my god, tequila.

The other three pick up their shot and a slice of lemon, lick the back of their hand, pour on a small amount of salt, then look at me expectantly. I reluctantly do the same.

'Right, lick, slam, drink, suck,' says Dicky.

We all lick the salt, slam the tequila, drink it back in one, then suck the lemon.

'Oh my God, that's disgusting.' I can't help but contort my face. They all laugh and Margot says, 'You'll get used to it, darling.'

'I'm not sure I want to.' An involuntary shudder ripples through my body and they all laugh.

Jackson walks onto the stage, looking very handsome in a white cowboy hat, jeans, and a white shirt, bright enough for any Persil ad. 'Good evening, everyone! We want to get this party started, but before we do, I've heard today that Wilf's funeral will be in two weeks. I've been led to believe that the hold-up is because of the undertakers being busy. As you all know, the wake is being held here for him, and I know you will all want to pay your respects. So, without further ado, I would like you all to raise a glass to our good friend Wilf.'

Everyone raises their glasses and in unison toast, 'To our good friend, Wilf!'

Jackson waits a beat before giving a little cough, 'Don't be shy, it's entertain yourselves tonight with karaoke! Okay, Big Dave, thanks for doing the music for us. We all appreciate it, don't we folks?'

Everyone claps, cheers, and whistles.

'Thank you, I'll kick us off with the one and only song I can sing half decently, and as it's a full moon party, it's quite fitting.'

Jackson goes to the side of the stage and picks up a guitar. He expertly plays and sings 'Bad Moon Rising'. Wow, this guy has talent! I'm guessing he has done it a few times before because everyone in the garden sings along raucously.

I am starting to feel a bit fuzzy headed as the shots keep on coming. Looking around at the people singing and laughing makes me realise that I haven't had such a good time in years!

There's a raffle for the local playgroup, and the

prizes are an hilarious mix of things you would never want to win, like a really ugly vase, an extra-large tracksuit, and a giant stuffed bear that's bigger than Jackson, but as it's for a good cause, everyone digs deep.

When the raffle is over, Jackson takes to the stage once more. 'We've got a rare treat for you tonight. Our very own Dicky has agreed to give us a song.' Cheers come from the crowd, and Dicky takes a deep breath and climbs the couple of steps onto the stage.

Dicky sings Dr Hook, 'Sharing the Night Together'. Her voice is husky and sexy, not too shabby at all. As she sings, she glances at me a few times, and my heart skips a beat, and my stomach does a roll, similar to that tingle when going over a humped bridge at speed. I feel myself blush, and Margot elbows me in the ribs.

'What?' I say, although I know what.

'Oh nothing, darling.' She takes a sip of her drink, and I notice her exchange a look with Stella.

I am having the most wonderful time, and I feel amazing, partly due to the tequila, partly due to how much I'm loving my new life.

They all try to get me to sing karaoke, but I emphatically decline. I wish I had Jackson's confidence and dare to walk onto the stage with *my* guitar and belt out a few numbers ... but I would literally pee myself with nerves.

'Okay, leave her alone... for now.' Dicky winks at me. 'I'll go get us all another round, same again everyone?'

While Dicky is at the bar, one of the staff brings me a drink over. It's a martini. I don't like martinis. Tony used to get me a martini whenever we went out, said it made me look sophisticated. Twat.

'The guy at the bar asked me to bring you this,' she says.

'What guy at the bar?' I stand up, trying to look through the back doorway.

The waitress does the same. 'Oh, he appears to have gone.' She shrugs and goes to walk away.

'Wait, who is it? What did he look like?' Please God, this can't be happening.

'Sorry, I don't know, I think he's a tourist. I've never seen him before.' She shrugs again and walks back inside.

My heart sinks, as there is only one person I know who would buy me a martini. Too much of a coincidence to be anyone else.

I feel a rising panic, and my phone beeps, telling me I have a text message: *Enjoy your drink.*

'Are you alright, darling? You've gone awfully pale.' Margot is talking to me, but everything is swimming in front of my eyes, and all the voices seem to be getting louder. Margot puts her hand on my arm, which jolts me, forcing me to answer.

'Erm, no, not really, I feel very sick all of a sudden. Would you please excuse me, I have to go home, please apologise to Dicky for me.' I really don't want to spoil everyone's night with my tales of woe, so I almost run from the garden.

I feel so frightened on the short walk home that I stick to the footpath that isn't as secluded as the beach. I keep looking over my shoulder and jumping at every little noise. It isn't him; it can't be. Just a coincidence.

When I get back to my cottage, I lock myself inside, checking every window is closed, shutting the curtains, and bolting the doors. My mind is racing from fear that Tony has somehow tracked me down and is now playing a cat-and-mouse game with me (me being the bloody mouse, obviously). Well, tonight has taken a turn for the worst, that's for sure. I was enjoying some time with Dicky and the flirting between us. After tonight, I really think she might like me, as in, *really* like me. Not that I will act on this, of course. I know my mum isn't here, but I still wonder what she would think about everything I do. I want to make her proud of me. I've not done anything so far to achieve that, though.

Lying in bed the next morning, I text Jackson to say I won't be in today, as I've got a stinking cold. I feel terrible about letting him down and lying. He's been so good to me.

As I get out of bed, my phone beeps, alerting me of a text. I'm almost afraid to look at it, in case it's him. But it's not. It's a text from Jess calling me a twat for leaving her behind the bar on her own. This makes me smile. Quickly followed by another saying: *Cold my arse! Is that what you call a hangover??*

I wish I had gone in and told the truth, told him that I think my steaming piece of shit of a husband has found where I am, and that I'm afraid to go out.

I feel a bit shaky, even a little unsafe. I had started to build a nice life for myself, and now I feel like my happiness is like sand trickling through my fingers. What a fucking fucker! I love my job and Jackson and Tammy. And to repay them, I have lied and let them down. When I first arrived, I told Jackson about Tony cheating on me, but I missed out all his controlling behaviour and how I walked on eggshells my whole married life for fear of offending or upsetting him in any way.

Thinking of this, anger fills me, making me feel braver. So, I take a deep breath, wash my face, put on some mascara, brush my hair, and start along the beach path. I am going to tell the truth. I'm going to tell Jackson I lied and get myself back behind that bar (if he forgives me, of course). I refuse to let Tony ruin everything.

As I'm stomping along with a determined stride, I hear my name being called. I recognise the voice immediately. It stops me dead in my tracks. On wobbly legs, I turn around and see Tony standing behind me. Oh my god, he must have been following me!

'Joanna, please just listen a minute.' His voice is wheedling, not like him at all.

'It was you at the bar last night, wasn't it? And you have been in my cottage, haven't you? You broke in! I should've known it was you when my glass ballerina had been knocked over.'

'Will you just listen to me a minute, Joanna?' True to form, he's getting agitated, his voice has an edge so sharp, it could cut.

'You have nothing to say to me that I want to hear, to be frank.' I try to walk on, but he steps in front of me, blocking the path.

'Just fucking listen, will you?'

'You are shagging my best friend—no—my only friend. Just fuck off, Tony, just leave me alone.'

He grabs my arms, digging his fingers into my skin. 'I want you to come home, Joanna, I'm no good without you. The house is a mess, I'm a mess, just come home. I forgive you.' I can smell whisky on his breath, and he's swaying slightly, which makes my stomach roll with disgust.

'You forgive me? You forgive me? What for? Julie not what you thought she was, eh? All the excitement gone now that you're not sneaking around behind my back?' I try to shrug him off, but he tightens his grip.

'Fucking get off me!'

I sound braver than I feel, but anger is overriding my fear. I swear to God, if we were up on the cliff, I would fucking push the wanker off!

'I did not break into that hovel you call home. I walked in through the back door. You really should lock it. You've always been too trusting.' He releases me and smirks. Adrenaline is coursing through me, and I'm literally fizzing with anger.

'And I forgive you for sneaking off like that! Julie is a friend, nothing more. You always overreact to everything, Joanna.' He's getting louder, and I want to take a step back, but I stand my ground.

'Don't treat me like an idiot. I saw the text messages between you.' His face looks shocked, but only fleetingly.

'Okay, look, she meant nothing, nothing to me at all.'

'Well, she did to me! And you have nothing to forgive me for, Tony, nothing at all. I did nothing wrong, never have. But I don't need you. I'm happy here! I finally have a life, and that doesn't, and will never, include you!'

A man and his dog are walking towards us, so he grabs me again and wraps me in a bear hug before whispering into my ear, 'I'm warning you, you bitch, you better come home because if you don't...'.

The dog walker goes by and says, 'Morning.' This gives me some courage, so I push him off as hard as I can. He releases me, his face puce with rage. 'I'm sorry, Jo, please just wait...'.

'Alright there, love?' The dog walker takes a step back towards us.

'Yes, yes, thank you, I will be.'

He nods and walks on, albeit slowly.

'I've filed for a divorce.' I haven't yet, but I want him to know that there is no chance of me returning to him. Anyway, it's the next thing on my to do list. 'I'm never coming back, Tony. You see, what you don't seem to get, is that I don't even like you; I hated my life with you. I was lonely and bored all the time, and you are a bully. If you ever come near me or my home again, I will call the police. I will Tony. I will tell them what a bully you are, and while I'm at it, I'll tell all of your mates as well. You might not be so popular then, so fuck off and don't come back, just fuck off!'

The look of disbelief on his stupid face almost makes me laugh out loud.

I walk back towards my cottage on very shaky legs. I want to run, but I don't want to give him the satisfaction. I just want to lock myself inside my cottage and shut all the curtains. I'll explain everything to Jackson tomorrow. I look back over my shoulder to make sure he isn't following me. In the distance, I can see a person that looks a lot like Dicky walking in the opposite direction. But it can't be; otherwise, she'd have seen me and come over to me, surely.

CHAPTER 7
STAND BY ME – BEN E KING

The next day, I arrive at work early, as I want to be open and honest about what has been happening with me. I find it really hard telling Jackson and Tammy that I didn't have a cold and wasn't even ill at all. The last thing I want them to think is that I'm a liar and can't be trusted.

We are all sitting around one of the pub tables with a cup of tea. Me, Jackson, Tammy, and Jess. Once I finished telling them everything, there's a silent pause for a few seconds, and I think I'm in trouble, and I'm struggling not to cry. Worries swirl around my head as I wonder whether Jackson will fire me, or whether he'll even believe me.

Jackson is the first to speak. 'Right, sunshine, I, or should I say we, will not have you frightened in your own home. We will not have you too frightened to come to work either. If that sorry excuse for a man turns up again, you call me, okay? I can be with you in the blink of an eye, day or night. I'll put the fear of God into him if needs be.'

Tammy is nodding enthusiastically. 'He will, you know. He hates bullies, seen a few off from this bar over the years, haven't you, love?'

'Aye, I have, and I will continue to do so, can't stand men who bully women, or bully anybody come to that.'

As relief washes over me, I suddenly feel drained of energy. I bury my face in my hands and start to cry. Tammy jumps up and puts an arm around my shoulders, making shushing noises and trying to sooth me.

Jess, obviously, has something to say. 'I think we should go find him and kick his head in!'

'Thank you, thank you so much, all of you. I don't think it'll be necessary to kick his head in, Jess, but thanks for the offer." I laugh. "I don't think, well, I hope he's gone. For the first time in ten years, I stood up to him, and I feel good about it actually. He looked as shocked as hell.' I laugh because to be honest, that look of shock on his stupid fucking face has made me feel stronger and more determined than ever.

'Good for you, proud of you, but how did he get into your cottage? Was a window broken or anything?' Tammy frowns.

'No, to be honest, it's my own fault, I left the back door unlocked.'

'You did what?' Tammy is shaking her head at me.

'Well, there is no easy access round the back, is there? So I thought it'd be okay.' Looking around at their incredulous expressions, I hold my hands up. 'Before you say it, I lock it every time I leave the house now.'

'Good, I should think so.' Tammy gives me a stern look.

'I told him I would call the police, and I bloody will. He wouldn't want that; it wouldn't go with the Mr Nice Guy image he puts on for everyone else.' I try to smile, but it wobbles slightly.

'Dicky came in, and said she'd seen you with a bloke on the path. She said she thought it was your husband. I didn't think anything of it, or I would've told Jackson.' Tammy gives me an apologetic smile.

'Wha—'

She interrupts me, 'Look hun, you look a bit shaken up, so why don't you have today off, eh? We'll manage without her won't we?' Tammy looks from Jackson to Jess, who both nod their heads.

I don't think the customers will get the best from me today, so I do just that. I'm pottering around my garden, thinking about Dicky. Why didn't she come over? Why wouldn't she come to help me? I guess she's pissed off that I left the Full Moon party early. But I've not got the energy to think about that right now.

I'm digging one of the borders and my thoughts turn to Tony. I guess Julie wouldn't dance to his tune because that didn't last long. Unless he's just hedging his bets, and she's at home waiting for him. Funny really, I told her often enough what he was like. She obviously didn't believe me; either that or she thought he would be different with her. That's what thought did, you two-faced bitch. I wonder if she's gone crawling back to her husband, who, by the way, is soft enough to forgive and forget. Do you know what? Why am I even giving them headspace? Enough, no more. I'm not going to let him spoil what I have here or take up any more of my time. I take my phone out and google the contact information for some local solicitors.

Over the next few days, I distract myself by putting all of my energy, when I'm not working, into my cottage and garden. Margot's painting looks absolutely amazing over the fireplace. It really catches the eye, and when the sun shines through the window, it lights it up, drawing the eye to it and gives the illusion that you are looking through a window instead of at a painting. I am very proud of how it's all turning out. The bathroom and kitchen have a fresh lick of white paint, which has brightened it up to no end. I have moved some of the furniture around to create some space. Moving the bed had the largest impact (no mean feat, I can tell you), so it is now facing the window. When the curtains are open, I can lie in bed and look over the bay. It never ceases to impress and please me. I asked Jackson to fit some heavy-duty bolts to my doors. I know someone could get in if they really wanted to, but it makes me feel safer.

The garden is looking less like a wilderness because I've finally gotten my hands on some tools! Jackson asked Kieron to drop off a spade, fork, lawnmower, shears, and secateurs. Kieron offered to help me, but I declined his kind offer, as I have been looking forward to putting my stamp on my little garden for weeks. He looked relieved, to be honest.

I want to be able to sit out here, so I need to find a little table and chairs for my little slabbed patio area. I love eating outside and listening to the birds. Hopefully, I won't get attacked by seagulls! They are very brave here, and I have witnessed them doing a kamikaze dive to nick food from unsuspecting people outside the Stern. Entertaining to watch, but not really the image of tranquillity I have in mind.

My biggest worry is that I could be doing all this for nothing. I really need another job. I need to get out there and have a good look. What I'll do, I do not know, but I worry that, when my savings are all gone, I won't be able to afford to stay here, and that would break my heart.

I've started planting, and I am up to my elbows in muck when there is a knock on my door. It makes me jump, and my heart hammers in my chest, probably at the prospect that it might be Dicky. It feels like ages since I've seen her. I've been too busy to go to the café much, and when I did, she wasn't there. I sent a text saying I wanted to talk to her, but she blue ticked me! She didn't strike me as the sensitive type.

I walk through the house, wiping my hands down my jeans and open the door, but it's not Dicky. It is Vicky, my sister. Oh, for fuck's sake, here we go. I guess I'm in for another argument.

'Are you coming in then?' I say after a few seconds of just standing looking at each other. She always looks the same. A proper Stepford wife is our Vicky. Nice house, nice car, nice husband, thin as a rake, and never a hair out of place. Tut.

'Hello Joanna.' She looks me up and down. Her voice is a bit clipped, and this annoys me. 'Of course I'm coming in. I didn't drive all this way to stand on your doorstep, did I?'

I tut and lead her through to the kitchen, and I wash my hands. 'Do you want tea, coffee, or wine?'

'I'll have wine if you're having one, please.'

'It's five o'clock somewhere.' I say, using my dad's old expression and she almost smiles, almost. I pour two glasses of white wine and guide her through to the lounge. She looks around, and I can't tell if she likes what she sees or not. Her face remains set in a scowl.

'You've clearly spoken to Tony to have found your way here then?'

'Yes, he's very upset, Joanna. He wants you to come home. He holds no animosity towards you. He said you threatened him with the police! I don't know what's got into you, I really don't.' She takes a sip of wine and does a little shudder. Not what she's used to, I should imagine; she makes me want to knock the glass out of her hand.

I swallow down my anger and a mouth full of wine. 'Okay, I was hoping you might have come to show me some support. You should be on my side; you are my sister after all.' She tries to interrupt, but I stop her with my hand. 'If you had any kind of sisterly relationship with me, Vicky, you would know that Tony is a bully. He has made my life a misery for years. Bet he didn't mention the fact that he's been shagging Julie, did he? No? I didn't think so. This is my home now, I love it, and if you want a relationship with me, Vicky, you can just bloody well pick a side. If that side is Tony's, then you can just fuck off.'

I'm out of breath, and my heart is hammering by the time I've finished, partly because I don't speak to Vicky like that (well, not since we were kids) and partly because it feels good to finally say it.

She squints at me and several seconds go by in stunned silence (on both our parts).

'Why didn't you ever tell me any of this, Joanna?'

'I have tried, Vic; I have tried loads of times. You never listened. You think the sun shines out of Tony's arsehole. I don't blame you, he can be all charm, generosity, and fun. Well, he isn't like that at home. Not one bit. It got to the point where I couldn't even think for myself. I daren't think for myself. Then, when I found out he was shagging my only so-called friend, something snapped in me. Do you know she hasn't even tried to call or text me? No apology or fuck all.'

Tears are running down my face, and I'm not sure why, but Vicky is crying too. She wipes her eyes with a very white cotton hankie she's fished from her designer handbag. Who even carries proper hankies these days?

We sit in the lounge, and I go on to tell her what some of my life was like. Not all of it, obviously, or it would take a week. But enough to let her know that the Tony she knows isn't the Tony I lived with for ten years!

'So, there you have it. My miserable life in a nutshell.'

'I'm sorry,' she whispers.

What? Am I hearing this right? Did she just say sorry to me?

'I'm sorry,' she repeats. 'I've been a shit sister, haven't I?'

'We drifted apart, Vic. That's on both of us, not just you. We moved in different circles, and to be honest, I felt like you didn't want me around. I didn't fit into your friendship group, and I didn't want to either. We just had very different lives, that's all. Plus, when we did call round, it always felt like you preferred Tony's company to mine. You fell hook, line and sinker for that charade of his. Not only you, though, everybody did. He's very good at it.'

'Is that how you felt, Jo? Well, I'm sorry, I mean it, I am. I wish we could start this visit again. Hold on.' She gets up, grabs her handbag and coat, and goes out of the front door, slamming it behind her. What the hell just happened?

Hearing a loud knock on the door, I jump up to answer it. She's standing there in her coat with her arms stretched wide. 'Jo! So good to see you!' She gives me a bear hug and breezes by me. 'So glad you've left that tosser, I always thought you were too good for him!' She laughs, and it makes me laugh out loud.

'That's more like it, eh?' she says whilst topping our glasses up.

'Yes, Vic, that's more like it.'

'I want us to be friends, not just sisters. We were closer when we were younger, weren't we?' She passes a very full glass to me.

I do a little snort at this because I can't remember being that close, to be honest. I just remember fighting a lot. But I swallow a snarky remark. 'Yeah, we were dead close.' I take a sip and look at her over the top of my glass, and we both laugh.

'Sarky cow.'

We finish the bottle, then another. We talk for hours, and we are very drunk and swing between tears, laughter, and back again. The strange thing is, I feel really good about this impromptu bonding session with my sister and find I'm really glad that she came. I'm glad she wants to have a relationship with me. I'm glad she knows the truth about my life and about Tony, but more importantly, I'm glad I have her as a friend. The only friend I have outside of Meadow-Cliff Bay.

She tells me more about her life and marriage than she ever has before.

'I know you won't believe me, but my life isn't as perfect as I try to make everyone believe. I get lonely a lot of the time because James works long hours. And as far as my friends are concerned, well, let's just say, I wouldn't tell them my innermost thoughts. If I did, I probably wouldn't be invited back.' She gives a wry smile.

'You missed your calling as an actress then, Vic.' I smile to show I'm only messing as she looks down and dabs her eyes with her hanky.

'The worst part is that we've been trying for a baby for a very long time, yet every month when I get my period, I cry and go back to bed, the longing is unbearable.' I hug her tight until the tears stop.

'Have you had tests? Considered IVF?'

'Yes, well, we saw a fertility doctor, and apparently, there is no reason why we haven't conceived. I just worry that we're running out of time.' She sniffs and gulps down her wine.

Whilst we are having a heart to heart, I decide to tell her about Dicky, about how I thought I was falling for her, but that it's ridiculous. I even tell her how she's suddenly gone cold on me, so it probably isn't going to come to anything. I thought she would be all judgey and disapproving. But, to my surprise, she really isn't.

'Why is it ridiculous, Jo? If you like this woman, perhaps you should be a bit more obvious. I know you.' She wags her finger. 'I bet you're giving her mixed signals, so she doesn't know where she stands with you. Ask her out or something, what's the worst that can happen?'

I can think of a few things actually, but I keep them to myself.

Standing and moving around the room, she picks up my guitar. 'I see you've brought Martin. Come on, give us a song, for old times' sake?' She passes it to me.

'It's a bit late, isn't it?'

'Sod the neighbours! Let them hear how talented you are!'

Bloody hell.

I quickly tune up, then I play 'Stand by Me' by Ben E King. We both sing along, loudly, and it takes me back to when Mum and Dad were alive, and we'd often sit around singing. I love it, and it feels like a perfect end to the evening.

I yawn, suddenly feeling bone-weary. It's funny how talking can exhaust you, isn't it? The wine probably helped too, I suppose.

I look at the time, and it's 2:00 a.m. 'Bloody hell, look at the time! I haven't got a spare room. It's only a one-bed cottage, but the bed's a double, so you can share with me.' I smile at her.

"Okay, great, I've already texted James, to let him know I'm stayiny. Better be no farting, mind!" She laughs. "You were such a farter as a kid."

We jostle each other as we climb the stairs on wobbly, drunken legs.

When we're in bed, she says, 'Turn over, I don't want you breathing in my face.' I tut, turning my back to her. To my surprise, she snuggles up to me. 'It's beautiful, your cottage, I love it, and you're beautiful too and I love you...'. She's gently snoring before she's finished her sentence.

Vicky leaves for home the next morning with a promise to come and see me more often. When we hug goodbye, it feels real and not that air-kissing thing she usually does.

As I stand waving her off, I feel happy that we have patched our relationship up but sad that we have wasted years not really talking properly, not really understanding each other when we could have been good friends. Oh well, look to the future, Jo, not the past. 'I bet you're happy about this turn of events, aren't you, Mum?' I look up to the sky, and I know she's smiling.

CHAPTER 8
IN THE LIVING YEARS –
MIKE & THE MECHANICS

It's the day of Wilf's funeral, and it's all hands to the pump, getting the Stern spick and span. Keiron and Steph are bickering about the food preparation in the kitchen. However, everything that comes out of that kitchen is lovely, and in fairness, Keiron is a perfectionist, hence the bickering.

I'm cleaning the bar, and I see Jess sneak over to the buffet table, which is set up in front of the fireplace. She quickly looks from side to side, then peels back some cellophane and slides an egg and cress sandwich out. She catches me looking at her, so she holds it up, waggles it and says, 'starving' before carrying on. She moves onto the sausage rolls as Keiron brings another tray of food in, shoving a whole one into her mouth. 'I saw that, Jess!'

'Wha...?'

I turn away so that Keiron doesn't see me laughing.

Noticing the time, I pull her towards the front door before she devours the whole buffet. 'Hang on! I haven't finished my makeup yet!' She sprays me with flaky pastry, and successfully shakes me off.

'See you at the church then.' I can't be late, or even nearly late. I get stressed and start to sweat at the mere thought of it. So, I'm leaving her to it.

As I step onto the street, the funeral procession slowly weaves through the crowd and towards the church. People line the road, eager to make Wilf's final journey an unforgettable one. Old men with bowed heads hold their caps in their hands, and old ladies are dabbing their eyes, as the hearse goes by, I join the back of the procession. I feel a bit silly on my own, so I just keep my head down, looking at the ground in front of me.

The little church is absolutely choc-a-block with standing room only. There are enough flowers to fill the Royal Albert Hall, showing how well thought of old Wilf was. There are flower arrangements shaped like tractors, pigs, and a pint of beer from all of us at the Stern. On the coffin is a tribute of blue flowers that simply reads, 'DAD'. I don't know why, but that one makes me feel the saddest of all. Richard sits on the front pew by himself. His head is bowed, and I feel quite sorry for him.

I look around for a seat, but they are all taken, so I stand to the side of the last pew. Luckily, Tammy and Jackson are sitting at this pew, both of them giving me a tight-lipped smile. They shuffle along a bit so that I can squeeze in next to them. Jess comes in last (obviously), and I wave to her to come and sit by me. She ignores me and carries on looking around. I stand and watch as she spots Richard. With quick steps, she walks down the aisle and slides into the pew next to him. I can't believe her brass neck. I watch as he does a small frown at her, but she nods at him and smiles, and to my surprise, he nods and smiles back. Being at an angle, I see him mouth, 'Thank you.' She'll do anything for a shag, that one.

We start by singing 'Amazing Grace', and the Vicar talks fondly about Wilf's long life in the bay.

Then Richard takes to the pulpit and clears his throat. He looks very smart in a black suit and tie. His hands shake a little as he unfolds a piece of paper.

'My dad liked this poem. He read it at my mum's funeral. Some of you may remember that.' He looks around with a pale, drawn face, and in a faltering voice, he reads the poem, 'Do Not Stand at My Grave and Weep'. Then he continues, 'Thank you all for coming to pay your respects today. My dad would have loved the fact that the church is so full.' He pauses, and there's smiles and nods from the congregation. 'He loved his life here in the bay, and true to his word, he never left it. When mum passed away, I was worried that he would be lonely, but because of so many of you, that wasn't allowed to happen. I would like to take this opportunity to thank you all for the love and friendship you showed him.'

Jackson turns and looks at me, pulling a 'well I never' face.

I can't help myself; I keep looking at the back of Dicky's head. She is sitting close to the front with her mum and Stella. As everyone follows the coffin into the graveyard, I try to make eye contact with her, but she is looking down, and I can tell she has been crying. I still haven't had a chance to talk to her. Hopefully, I will today.

Despite what he said about getting straight back to the city, Richard comes to the pub after the service. He stands on his own at the bar, people talking to him intermittently to pass on their condolences. I notice Jess talking to him whenever she can. They seem to be getting on well. He nods a lot and smiles as she chatters. Jess could brighten anyone's day, I'm sure.

We're very busy behind the bar, so we don't get a lot of time to chat with anyone.

'I've got to head off now, but I just wanted to say thank you and ask how much I owe you for the buffet, Jackson?'

'Nothing at all, Richard. We were glad to do it for Wilf.'

'Well, if you're sure, that's very good of you, thank you.' He turns to Jess, giving her a sad smile. 'Thank you, Jess, you've really helped me get through this day.' He kisses her on the cheek and leaves.

'Well, that's that, then.' She sighs heavily. 'The last I'll see of him, I bet.'

'Oh, I don't know, Jess,' grumbles Jackson. 'He'll be back to sell off that farm before long. You mark my words.'

Jess purses her lips and frowns in disapproval, but very wisely, she does not try to stick up for Richard and keeps her mouth shut.

Dicky has only been to the bar once, and Jackson got there before me. I swear to God, I felt like rugby tackling him to the ground to get there first so that she had to talk to me.

We've made eye contact a few times, but the smile wasn't the warm, sexy one she usually treats me to. In fact, her eyes look sad. I guess losing Wilf has hit her harder than I thought. I must check on her when I get a moment.

A few hours later, the punters thin out quite a lot, so Jackson tells me and Jess to knock off. We both grab a glass of wine and thankfully go and sit down.

'My feet are killing me.' Jess has removed her shoes and is unashamedly rubbing her toes.

'High heels might have been a bad choice when you're on your feet all day, Jess.' I laugh.

'They show off my legs. I've got some trainers in the back,' she says, still rubbing her feet.

'Very shapely legs too. I wonder whose benefit those heels were for?' I say, raising my eyebrows, then I add, 'Did Richard mention selling the farm?'

'No, he didn't. He was very nice, actually. I felt sorry for him. He's really sad about his dad. I know folks around here don't think so, but he did love him.'

'He should've shown it then when he was alive,' interjects Jackson as he leans over to wipe our table.

I shake my head at Jess, mentally warning her not to start with him.

'Anyway, how's you? Any lovely woman with dark curly hair on the horizon?' I give her a look that clearly shows my shock.

'I'm not blind, you know, or stupid!' She laughs. 'I've seen the way you look at each other when we go to the café.'

'Yes, well, I was interested and so was she, I think,

but now she isn't. I know she is upset about Wilf, but I feel like she's avoiding me.' I pull a sad face.

'Ah, do you want me to have a word? Find out what's going on?'

'No, Jess! Absolutely not, I mean it. Just stay out of it, please. I'll ask her myself when I get the chance. I don't want you sticking your nose in.'

'So you don't want me to say my mate fancies you?'

I laugh and say, 'No thank you, don't you go making me look even more uncool than I do already.'

She sees me looking around the pub.

She laughs as she stands to go and get her trainers. 'She went ages ago.'

CHAPTER 9
RIDE THE WILD SURF –
JAN & DEAN

Following Wilf's funeral, the village has a short period of normality, which is short lived because Hillside Quay hosts an annual surfing contest. Meadow-Cliff Bay acts as an over-spill for all the surfers and their companions who couldn't find accommodation in the town's many hotels and B&Bs, meaning the B&B, the Stern, and the caravan park are booked up with people. The beach and sea here get crowded too, as they also do their practice surfing on Meadow-Cliff beach. I'm looking forward to watching and hopefully learning a few tips and tricks.

During our lunch time shift, Jess is literally hopping around with excitement. 'We'll definitely pull this weekend Jo! I'll have the surfer dudes, and you can have the surfer, erm ... dudettes!'

'Plural? More than one in a weekend, eh?' I laugh. 'And what makes you think I wouldn't want a surfer dude, Jess?'

'Who are you trying to kid, me or you? If my gaydar

was switched on, when I walk towards you it would be going beep ... beep ... beep ... beep, beep, beep,' she says this while walking closer to me, making me laugh out loud. 'Anyway, we are young, free, and single. Last year, I was fighting them off with a stick, except I didn't have a stick, and I didn't fight too hard, if truth be told.' She laughs.

'I can imagine.' I chuckle.

'You obviously haven't always been into women then, Jo?' Jess is sticking up cardboard surfboards and palm tree decorations to just about everything, to the point where I daren't stand still too long.

'Erm, yes and no, and stop sticking palm trees everywhere and come and have a cuppa.' I put two mugs of tea and a box of chocolate fingers on the table.

'In actual fact, I didn't think about it too much until I got here." I laugh.

'Until you clapped eyes on the delectable Dicky.'

'I guess so,' I say, taking a sip of tea.

'Oh, right, anyway, I bet you'll see quite a few this weekend that you'll find interesting!' She takes a drink of tea and pops a whole chocolate finger in her mouth.

'I doubt it very much. I'm not the kind of person who is easily attracted to people, and I'm definitely not a one-night stand kinda girl. It's just not me.'

'Okay, Miss Prim and Proper!' She flicks my arm, quite hard.

'Ouch, no offence meant, Jess! It's just that I'm a romanticist. I don't want a doofer, and I definitely don't want to be someone else's doofer. I like seeing someone, having dates, getting to know them better, getting closer.' This makes me think of Dicky, and I get up with a sigh.

Jackson has booked a local band, which I have on good authority as being excellent. Jess has asked for tonight off, as she wants to party with the surfer crowd. Thanks a bunch, Jess.

Tonight is mental in the bar. I literally do not stop for six hours straight. The band, just as promised, is excellent, and I'm glad they are booked again for Saturday night. I thought it would be all Beach Boys' music, as it's surf season, but it isn't. It's a really good mix of new and old stuff, and the place is jumping.

Jess' doing the rounds, is getting up close and personal with at least three different blokes, and that's only the ones I notice. It could, of course, be more. When I nip to the loo, she is snogging a particularly handsome guy. As I pass by, she winks at me over his shoulder. I give her a thumbs up. You go, girl!

I can't help but look for Dicky because I have made up my mind to find out why our friendship seems to be fizzling out, but she hasn't come in. Shit.

The next morning, I wake up early, and since I can't get back to sleep, I decide to watch the sun rise from the beach. As I step onto the sand, the sun is just peeking above the horizon. I stop to drink it in; it's spectacular. I hear a yap, then I notice Dolly digging and sniffing around in the sand. She spots me and comes running up, wagging her little tail.

'Hello Dolly.' I can feel a song coming on. I sit on the

sand and stroke her fluffy head, which makes her bark louder. I see Dicky surfing. She really is incredible. Perhaps she's practising for the surfing competition?

It is one of those mornings when you know it's going to be a beautiful. You just know the sun is going to burn off the sea mist, clearing the way for a warm and bright day. There's a smell in the air that only comes with a summer morning. It fills me with happiness, and I smile down at the little dog, tickling her under her chin. She sits contentedly next to me, and if I didn't know better, I would swear she is smiling up at me.

'Looks like you've made a friend.' Dicky walks towards us, water dripping from her hair. 'I'm glad you're here because I think I owe you an apology.' She peels the top of her wetsuit down slowly, showing off her brown toned body. Does she do that on purpose? She then sits next to me on the sand.

'Oh?' I sound too hopeful for my liking.

'Jess spoke to me, and she told me about the Full Moon party.' She wrings the water from her hair.

'Oh God, I told her not to stick her beak in. I was going to speak to you myself. I wasn't sure if you were avoiding me or just too upset about Wilf and needed some time alone.' I pick up a handful of sand and let it trickle through my fingers.

'Jess told me what had happened with your ex. I'm sorry, I came to see if you were okay the next morning, and I saw you hugging on the footpath in what I thought was a reconciliatory way.'

'Ah, no, the complete opposite actually.' Dolly jumps onto my knee, and I give her a cuddle.

'I know that wasn't the case now, so I'm sorry for jumping to the wrong conclusion and for being a twat.'

'You could have asked me, you know.' I feel a bit annoyed, and it shows in my voice, as it comes out harsher than I intended.

'I know, but I wanted to give you space, not complicate things for you, so I just thought it best to stay out of the way and give you a chance to think. I feel stupid and like I let you down a bit.'

'Do you, how?' I remove Dolly from my knee, and she starts digging in the sand again.

'I backed away when you needed a friend. I'm so mad at myself for turning back that day. I wish I had carried on towards you. I was so disappointed to see what I thought I saw, that I just had to get outta there.'

'Don't worry about it, it doesn't matter now; he's gone thank fuck, hopefully for good.'

'Are you okay?' She puts a hand on my arm.

'I am. I feel stronger now than ever, and I'm not scared anymore. I'm looking forward, not back. Fuck him.'

'Good.' She removes her hand, and I wish she hadn't.

We sit looking at the sea for a few minutes, then I carry on.

'My sister, Vicky, came to see me. Hopefully, she'll come back again soon. I think you'd like her.'

'Good, I'm glad. Will you be staying in the bay then?'

'There was never any question about me staying.'

'Good, I just thought, you know, when I saw you with him that you'd be going back with him.'

'Not a chance, Roberta; no, and never, in that order!'

She raises her eyebrows, 'Roberta?'

'Yes, I'm hammering a point home.' I smirk at her, and she smiles back, the smile that gives me butterflies in my belly.

I could kill Jess. I told her not to stick her nose in, but at the same time, I want to twirl her around and kiss her.

'You practising for the competition?'

She laughs. 'No, I just do it for fun and to keep fit. Have you seen the pros? They are amazing. I'd get laughed out of the competition.'

'Well, you look pretty amazing to me.' I hold her gaze, and I feel a little burst of excitement.

I spend most of the morning up the coast in Hillside Quay, watching the surfers. Dicky was right, they are amazing! How the hell they stay on the boards is a mystery to me. Imagine being that graceful, although, as far as a novice like myself can tell, Dicky isn't that far off.

Apparently, it's a cracking day for surfing. 'Offshore waves', whatever that means. They speak a different language that may as well be foreign to me.

I love watching and listening to them. If I thought I would get some tips about learning to surf, I was so wrong. They make it look as easy as riding a bike, but I know from previous experience, it really isn't. It's probably taken them their whole lives to get this good. I'm going to learn though, if I could catch just one wave, I'd be over the moon. Obviously, it'll have to wait until all these experts have buggered off.

I walk back along the cliff tops towards Meadow-

Cliff Bay. It is stunning. The sky is the most beautiful cloudless blue, and the sea is turquoise in the shallows, growing darker as it gets deeper. A few boats are bobbing about and some have little white sails. It's picture postcard beautiful. I even take pleasure in watching the seagulls too. Most people hate them and call them 'sky rats', but not me. Even when they wake me up with their distinctive cries before the crack of dawn, I really don't mind. The best alarm clock ever, in my opinion. It's hard to believe that this is England; I feel so lucky to be able to call this place my home. Thinking about this reminds me of my financial situation. I need to earn enough without eating into my savings because when they are gone, I'm up shit creek.

Since being here, I haven't really had the chance to walk over the cliffs. However, I make a pact with myself to embed this activity into my weekly routine. It is not only beautiful and peaceful, it's also great exercise. I am out of breath and sweating! All over the clifftop are thousands of little blue flowers. They look like meadow clary, a little bluish-purple flower I used to pick as a kid. This makes a lot of sense, as the café is called Clary's! I must ask Dicky or Margot about that.

They make the clifftop look like it is covered in deep blue water. A beautiful sight. I can see why Wilf wanted to hang on to this. What a shame that it may all disappear and a big hotel complex may be erected in its place.

I sit on the grassy cliff to admire the view and take a sip of water. What an amazing place to just sit and think. I let my mind drift for a while. It feels good to realise that I have very little to stress about. Money is tight, but if I can get another job, even part time, I could make it work. I don't need a fortune. I have no need to go anywhere. Everything I need and want is right here in this bay.

I looked at myself in the full-length mirror this morning, and I smiled at what I saw reflected back at me. I have a tan! I'm never going to get that Mediterranean colour Dicky has, but I'm happy with my sun-kissed look. I've lost some weight too. Must be all the gardening and walking I've been doing. I actually like how I look, which is a bit of a revelation to me. Good enough to wear short shorts! Who'd have thought it?

My mind drifts to Dicky (obviously), and I can't help but hope she is still interested in me. It felt like she was earlier this morning. I need to sort my mixed-up head out. One minute, I'm hoping she likes me, the next, I'm feeling apprehensive about a new relationship, especially one with a woman. God, even thinking about it gives me butterflies.

But, as Vicky said, what's the worst that can happen? Well, she could say she wants to just be friends. Embarrassing, but not the end of the world, is it?

'What do you think, Mum? Do you think she's interested in me?'

A gentle breeze floats across my face, which lifts my hair and feels like a soft kiss on the cheek. I'll take that as a yes then, Mum.

CHAPTER 10
TAKING CARE OF BUSINESS – BACHMAN TURNER OVERDRIVE

I am at the point where I need to find another job, or it won't be too long before I can't afford the rent and my other bills. This has been keeping me awake at night. There is nothing in the bay, as I've already tried everywhere. So, I'm off to Hillside to seek gainful employment. I am literally prepared to do anything!

I'm dressed for business and full of enthusiasm. I start off full of hope, trudging from shop to shop, café to café, asking to speak to managers, but after several hours of hearing 'Sorry we have nothing at the moment', I start to feel a little despondent, and I get really fed up.

Every sorry or shake of the head feels like a slap. Money worries can cast a big fat shadow over the brightest of days, can't they? What am I going to do? I've trawled the internet, and there's nothing within an hour's drive. I can't leave my cottage and the bay, and I bloody won't go back to Tony. I could go to our Vicky's, I suppose, if she'd have me. But that would mean leaving my new life and new friends. It's unthinkable! I'm sure they wouldn't let me leave anyway. Right, I need to get some positive thinking back! No one will want to employ a misery guts, will they?

I think I'll call it a day and have a rethink. Anyway, I need to get back to the bay to get ready for work. It's going to be another busy one, or so I'm told. I need to put on my game face and not let my worries show. Being behind a bar is a bit like being on stage, I have discovered, as I put on a smile no matter what. Teeth and tits as Jess would say!

CHAPTER 11

A WHITER SHADE OF PALE
– ANNIE LENNOX

I 'm looking forward to going to work tonight. I will put my money worries to the back of my mind for this evening. I'm going for the hippy/festival look (without the wellies).

Mm, what am I going to wear? I put on a frayed denim skirt that's short enough to show off my tan), yes. Where is that tie-dye T-shirt? Got it. Yep, that works. Hair up or down? Down, I fluff it up a bit. Wish I had time to curl it. I add a few fake flowers and weave them through it. Flat strappy sandals, which tie up my calves to finish the look. Ta-dah! Looking good, if I do say so myself.

This afternoon, when I mentioned the festival look I was going for, Jess insisted on us both having glitter on our cheeks in a curve that starts on our foreheads. I can feel the glue whenever I talk or smile, which is a little annoying, but she assured me I look cool. Who would've thought I would leave the house with so much skin on show and glitter! I smile as I think of what Tony would say about my appearance because he would hate it.

I feel cool actually, so sod it. My mum used to say you should be young when you are young, and late thirties isn't old, is it?

It's super busy in the pub, and although I have caught sight of Dicky, I haven't had much of a conversation with her, other than to take her order. Later, while I am collecting glasses and wiping down some tables, she says I look sexy, which makes my heart skip a beat or two, and my hips sway when I walk. She's with a few people from the surfing crowd, and they clearly know her well, as it's all banter and laughter whenever I look over at them. God, I love her laugh.

The band is good and they sing the kind of songs that make everyone want to dance and sing along. The band members are friends of Jackson's, and they force him onto the stage to perform.

He sings his favourite song, 'Bad Moon Rising', which everyone loves, then they keep him there for another. The whole place joins in on the echo as he sings 'Mustang Sally'. He's loving it, I can tell. This surfing crowd definitely know how to have a good time.

A very attractive girl asks me if she can buy me a drink. It throws me, and I don't know what to say for a second or two. Have I got 'potential lesbian' written across my forehead? I end up just smiling and saying, 'No thank you.' She is clearly just fishing, as I see her ask Jess, who immediately accepts. She does make me laugh.

When the punters thin out, Jackson pours me and Jess a large glass of wine, and we take it outside to the beer garden. The garden looks every bit as lovely as it did at the Full Moon party. All the lights just say 'summer holiday' to me.

'No surfer dude tonight, Jess?'

'Nah, not tonight. I thought there were slim pickings, to be honest. I'm saving myself for tomorrow night.' She rubs her hands together. 'The Saturday night is usually much busier as the surf competition will be over, so they won't have to worry about a hangover.'

'Makes sense. Oh yes, that reminds me, I thought I told you not to do any matchmaking between me and Dicky?' I give her what is supposed to be a stern look.

'Oh, come off it. If I had left it up to you two, you'd both be old women by the time you kissed and made up. Have you then?'

'Have I what?'

'Have you kissed and made up? Give me details. I've never been into women, but I would like to experience it vicariously through you.'

'Yes, everything is fine. We spoke this morning, in fact. But no, we haven't kissed, and you not being into women doesn't stop you from flirting with them, I have noticed.' I laugh.

'I like to keep my options open, never say never, that's my motto.' I think Jess' carefree attitude is rubbing off on me because that's exactly how I am feeling.

To my surprise, Dicky comes through the door into the garden. She makes a beeline for us and sits at our table. 'Can I get you two a top up?'

'No thanks, I'm outta here.' Jess slides from the bench and adds, 'Don't do anything I wouldn't do!'

I laugh, 'Sod off, Jess.'

At the same time Dicky says, 'Anything goes then!'

Dicky and I have another drink, and it goes straight to my head. I'm such a lightweight when it comes to drinking wine. This is not helped by the fact that I drink them fast, probably due to nerves and the fact that I haven't eaten much today.

As if she has read my mind, she asks, 'Are you hungry?'

'Yes, I am a bit.'

'Me too. Do you fancy grabbing some chips on the way back and eating them at mine?'

I hesitate, but only for a second. 'Yeah, lovely, just give me a few minutes to finish up here.'

I collect the glasses from the tables outside and load them into the glasswasher inside.

As I do a bit of litter picking outside, I can feel Dicky watching me, which makes me nervous and stirs up the butterflies in my belly.

'You've done enough now, pet. You can get off home." Jackson says as he enters the garden, and takes the bag of litter from me.

'Okay, goodnight!' I wave at Jackson as I walk over to see if Dicky is ready to go. She stands up immediately, and her smile sends little shock waves through me. Now that I have decided to let whatever happens happen, I feel jittery and nervous, like I'm going for an interview (minus the suit and add in sexual excitement). Okay, nothing like going for an interview, but you get the picture.

Thetresse chip shop is closing as we get there, but he wraps up a mixture of random stuff that's leftover, and we hurry to Dicky's flat above the café before it gets cold.

As soon as we walk through the door, Dolly bounds over, happy to see us. Well, happy to see Dicky really. Dicky's flat is small and a tad untidy. There are books on surfing and magazines piled on a little coffee table and on the floor, and items of clothing are draped over the back of the settee. The radiators are full of underwear, obviously put there to dry.

'Sorry about the mess,' she says as she quickly grabs all the clothing and disappears into what I assume is the bedroom.

'Thank God for that, I thought you'd been burgled.' I laugh, and she laughs too.

Dolly cannot contain her excitement and greets me like an old friend. She wags her tail so vigorously that her whole-body waggles from side to side.

I unwrap our parcel of chips, and he has added a battered sausage, a small fish, and a small pot of gravy to our original order.

Dicky laughs when she sees what we've got. 'Bless him. He always does this with the last customer of the day. He once gave me enough to feed a small army, so it went into the bin anyway, apart from a bit of fish for Dolly.'

We sit on the settee and pick at the chips. My hunger has gone and been replaced with excitement. I take off the batter and feed the sausage to a grateful Dolly.

'I need to take Dolly out for a wee. I won't be long, so don't go anywhere,' she says as she attaches Dolly's lead to her collar.

While she's gone, I take a proper look around the room.

Behind the battered old leather settee is a bookshelf full of old books and CDs, and I notice she has a varied taste in music. There's everything from Johnny Cash to Adele. There's a small coffee table and bare floorboards with a big blue rug in the centre. Two of the walls are bare brick and the other two have been plastered and painted an off-white colour. There are a few small paintings of the bay, obviously Margot's work. There are also a couple of photos of a pretty little girl. I imagine she is about two years old in one of them and a baby in the other. Is this her child? No, it can't be, I'd have met her by now. Maybe a niece? She's never mentioned having a brother or sister though. It could be Dicky when she was little, I suppose. I look closer to see if I can see any resemblance, but I can't. I'll have to ask her who she is.

The flat is charming and I like it. It makes you feel like you can put your feet up and chill without offending the owner.

Dicky and Dolly come back from their little walk, and Dicky pours more wine and puts on some music.

We chat, and she asks lots of questions and seems genuinely interested in the answers. She tells me how she came to own Clary's Café, which was gifted to her by Margot. She studied catering and was a singer in a band when she was much younger, which was called, 'She Devil'. We both laugh, and she looks embarrassed and quickly adds that she didn't pick the name for the band.

There's a pause while Dicky changes the music.

'Who is singing this?' I ask.

'It's Annie Lenox's "Whiter Shade of Pale". Do you like it?'

'Yes, I do. It's a sexier version than the "Procol Harum" one, isn't it?'

'That's the idea,' she says, treating me to that sexy smile again.

She takes hold of my hand and pulls me up. Her hazel eyes are looking into mine, almost as if she can read my thoughts. I want to look away, but I can't. I know how a rabbit caught in headlights feels now.

Dicky slowly pulls me to her, and we sway to the music. Her scent is musky and erotic. We move in time to the rhythm, and I can feel her warm breath on my face. As we dance slowly, she kisses me softly on my neck. I feel like I have been plugged into an electrical current.

I'm tingling all over, and although I feel nervous, I begin to unbutton her shirt, which falls from her shoulders to the floor, quickly followed by her bra. I kiss her again. 'You're beautiful.'

She pulls my t-shirt over my head and releases the clasp of my bra. Oh my god, I'm actually doing this!

She runs her fingers down my arm and a thunderbolt of desire shoots through me. The rest of our clothes follow in rapid succession.

We fall back onto the settee as she kisses me all over.

Her skin is so smooth, her lips so soft, and her long hair tickles me as she trails kisses down my body.

She is in no hurry as her tongue, lips, and fingers explore my whole body. She runs a line of little kisses up my inner thigh and as she licks me, she gently tugs on my nipples, and I explode in the most incredible orgasm of my life.

Full of nerves, but buoyed up by this incredible woman. I kiss and stroke her body. Her nipples are dark and hard, and she arches her back and moans as I lick them. I lick down her body, taking my time, loving the feeling of her against me and the fact that she's obviously enjoying it. Her breathing gets heavier and faster, and the sound of her coming almost makes me come again.

We lie together, letting our heartbeats slow down. 'That was amazing. You're an incredible lover,' I say, kissing her soft lips again.

'Right back at cha. I could so get used to you.' She pulls a throw from the back of the settee and covers us. We fall asleep, tangled together, right there. Me, with a happy smile on my face.

By the time morning rolls around, I'm in Dicky's bed. I remember Dicky waking me up in the middle of the night to move to the bedroom. It's a big comfy bed and smells of her. I could literally stay here all day.

I hear movement, so I open my eyes to find her standing before me, holding two mugs of tea, absolutely starkers. 'Well, this wake up call is the best ever!' I shuffle up the bed so that I'm in a seated position, and I take my tea from her as she gets back into bed beside me.

'Are you hungry? I'm sure I could rustle us something up.'

'Only for you.' I cringe at my cheesy line, but she doesn't react. She just takes my tea from me, puts it on the bedside table, and kisses me. I've never really been someone who enjoys morning sex, but as she takes me very slowly to the same heights as last night, I realise that I definitely am into morning sex after all. Who knew?

Her phone rings, and she leans over to retrieve it from the bedside table. 'I'm glad that didn't ring a few minutes earlier.' She looks at the caller ID, rolls her eyes, and whispers, 'sorry.' Then, she answers it, 'Buenos Dias, que tal?' She listens to the reply while slipping a robe on, mouthing sorry again as sits at the bottom of the bed 'Que aqui' cuando? Oh OK' si, necesito advertirle a mama. Te llamo mas tarde.'

She hangs up and I comment, 'Very impressive and sexy. I take it that was your dad?'

'Si, I mean yes, he's coming to see me, so I need to tell Mum. She hates it when he turns up out of the blue. How did you guess it was my dad?'

'I didn't guess exactly. Your mum told me your dad's from Spain, so when I heard all the Spanish, I assumed it was him. You glad he's coming?' I can't tell from her expression whether she's happy or not.

'I guess so. I want to see him, but I don't want him asking Mum for money or pissing her off. She's in a good place, and I don't want him mucking that up for her.'

'He speaks English, I take it?'

She laughs and says, 'Yes, of course, but he always says he wants to make sure I don't forget how to speak Spanish, so whenever we have a telephone conversation, it's in Spanish. He hates it when I get something wrong and corrects me all the time.' She smiles then says, 'Anyway, enough about him. What are your plans for today? It's the last day of the surfing competition, so I wondered if you would like to go to Hillside with me to watch it?'

'I can't, I'm afraid I'm working lunch time today, but I've got tonight off! We could meet at mine for a couple of drinks, then head out if you're up for that? God, look at the time, I've gotta go.' I jump out of bed and head to the bathroom.

'Sounds good to me,' she calls after me.

She kisses me as I'm leaving, and it's the kind of kiss that I have to tear myself away from before I change my mind and stay.

I head back to my cottage to shower and get ready for work, humming happily to myself the whole time.

CHAPTER 12
SWEET CHILD OF MINE – GUNS AND ROSES

'Someone had a good night, then?' You can't get much past Jess.

'Yes, a very good night, actually.' I grin, which is a mistake because then she's pecking at me for details.

'Spill! I want to know every detail. Leave nothing out. I'll get us a cuppa before we open up.'

I let her make us a brew, then we sit at our usual table, and she says, 'Well? Come on!'

'Sorry, Jess! I don't kiss and tell. All I will say is that I am a very happy woman and will definitely be going back for more.'

'Oh my god, you spoilsport! I would tell you!'

'I know you would—well you do—but I'm not you.' I laugh. And Jess sulks for the rest of the time it takes for her to drink her tea'

We are just finishing setting up the bar for lunch when Jackson shouts, 'Joanna! Jess! Come here a minute.'

He sounds stressed, so we take the stairs two at a

time. 'What's up?' Jess and I say at the same time as we burst into their sitting room..

Tammy is sitting on the settee, holding her round stomach.

'I think I'm in labour, but it's a bit early for that, so it could easily be a false alarm, but I've been getting contractions for a while now, and they're getting much stronger and closer together.' She looks far less worried than Jackson, who is pacing up and down the room.

Jess takes charge. 'Right, okay, Jackson, have you called the hospital? No? Well, do it now. Tell them you're coming in. Tammy, it's okay, you're only three weeks early, so the baby will be absolutely fine, I'm sure of it. Have you packed your hospital case?'

'Yes and no. Just the baby's things. I was going to do my stuff today, ironically.' Tammy looks at me and raises her eyebrows at the uncharacteristic sight of Jess taking control.

'No problem. Jo, can you help Jackson pack for Tammy?'

I have to take several items back out of the case that Jackson puts in. For example, little lace pants. 'She won't need these, Jackson.' I laugh, and I find some maternity underwear that is far more suitable for her. Luckily, Tammy had already bought and packed the toiletries for herself and the baby, or God knows what Jackson would have taken for her.

'What am I going to do about tonight? Oh my God, we're going to have a baby!' Jackson is flapping, which makes me laugh. 'It's okay, me and Jess will manage the bar, won't we, Jess?" I shout through to the sitting room.

'Yes absolutely, don't you worry about the pub. We'll

be fine. You just make sure you keep us informed every step of the way!'

Tammy is breathing through another contraction, which seems to be quite strong. We wait for it to pass before helping her down the stairs and into the car.

Jess and I stand on the roadside and wave them off, then I go back into the bar to start my shift.

'You did well there, Jess,' I say. 'Proper had it all under control. Proud of you, buddy.'

'Hey, there's more to me than meets the eye, you know!'

'I don't doubt it.'

'Jackson and Tammy will make such wonderful parents. I'm so happy for them. Please God, let them deliver this baby safely,' she says, placing coasters on the bar.

'This baby? What do you mean?'

'They've lost a couple of pregnancies in the past. They were heartbroken. Tammy said she didn't think she could live through anymore loss, so they stopped trying. Low and behold, that's when she fell pregnant. It's all been good so far this time. I can tell Jackson is anxious, though.'

'Oh my God, how awful for them! I feel more anxious now you've told me that! I owe them so much. I don't know what I'd have done if they hadn't helped me when I first got here. They really are salt of the earth, aren't they?"'

'Yes, they are. I was in the care system when I was young, bounced around from foster home to foster home. I was a bit of a tearaway, hard to believe, I know.' She laughs.

'Very hard to believe, as you're all sweetness and sunshine now.'

'Yes, anyway, Jackson and Tammy kind of took me under their wing. Gave me a job, helped me find my flat. I can't count how many times they've stepped in to help me. They are like my older brother and sister. I love em.'

'Ah, that's lovely Jess, it just makes me love them all the more. How did they meet?' I only ask because Jackson is a bit older, and he has a broad northern accent.

'Now that's a very romantic story that is best told by the two of them,' she says, heading into the kitchen.

The bar isn't too busy as the main surfing event takes place in Hillside Quay, so Jess and I check our phones every few minutes for any news from Jackson. Eventually, we get a text to say that Tammy's waters have broken, but she's doing okay. It appears that they will definitely meet their new addition sometime soon.

When I get a minute, I text Dicky to tell her the news about Tammy and also that I will be working tonight now, so won't be able to meet at hers. She sends loads of questions back about Tammy, and says she'll come to the bar later. I take out my phone, and google about having a baby three weeks early. It's not really classed as premature, so hopefully everything will be fine.

Dicky visits the bar in the early evening as the band is setting up. She is with some surfers, and they are all in high spirits.

Jess is very short with one of the girls as she serves her. 'Do you know her, Jess?' I ask, intrigued because I've never heard Jess be so unfriendly or dismissive to anyone before.

'Mm, it's Kathy, Dicky's ex. She isn't very nice. She treated Dicky like shit, so I don't like her much. She turns up now and again, usually to cause Dicky more heartache. I'm guessing she came back for the surf competition, but she could just as easily be here to mess with Dicky's head again.'

Oh God. She surfs, and she's gorgeous. She has that typical surfer look. Long blonde hair, nice figure, tanned, the whole fucking package. There's no way I can compete with that.

My stomach drops, and I feel hot. I can't help but look over in their direction, and she's standing very close to Dicky and smiling at her. When she speaks, she keeps touching Dicky's arm. This irritates me, and I can't help but feel worried, if I'm honest. They make a stunning couple. You know how you would put some people together if you had to pick them out of a line up? Well, that's what you'd do if Kathy and Dicky were in a line up. Deep fucking joy.

The bar is super busy, and me and Jess don't stop until almost closing time. Dicky and her friends have gone outside into the beer garden, which is good because I would've been watching her all night. Jealousy is not attractive to anyone, so I am determined to hide how I feel.

I check my phone, and I have a missed call from Jackson. I mention this to Jess, and she has a missed call too. Jess and I quickly go to the toilet, where it's quieter, and I call him back.

I have to try twice, as he doesn't pick up the first time.

I put my phone on loud speaker so that Jess can hear. 'Jackson, its Jo, we missed your call!'

'Hi Jackson,' Jess shouts in the background.

'Hello, you two. Well, I called to tell you the latest. We've got a baby girl! She's perfect.'

'Is she alright and is Tammy okay?' I ask.

'She's fine, weighs six pounds, six ounces, so she's not too small, although she looks tiny to me.' He chuckles. 'Tammy is fine. Just tired. She was a proper star. I'm so proud of her.' He sounds a bit choked up, bless him.

'Have you named her yet? Can I tell people?' Jess presses her head against mine, so that he can hear her..

I add, 'We understand if you want to do it yourself.'

'No, we haven't given her a name yet, and yes, you can tell our friends in the pub. I've called all the people closest to us and my folks up north, so go for it. I'm staying at the hospital tonight, so can you and Jess lock up properly? Oh, and I forgot to ask, is everything okay at the pub?'

'Of course, we'll lock up properly.' I tut. 'And yes, everything is absolutely fine, no issues at all. Congratulations to you both, I'm so happy for you. Give Tammy and baby no name a kiss from me and Jess, won't you?'

'Bye Jackson! Big hugs,' calls Jess.

Once I've hung up, I go up to the band. They have just announced it's their last number of the night, so I ask them to announce Jackson and Tammy's news.

Drum roll, please. 'Okay folks, big news for all of you who know Tammy and Jackson, they have had a lovely baby girl. Both mother and baby are doing well.'

The whole pub cheer and sings along as the band performs 'Sweet Child of Mine' by Guns N' Roses.

I'm not sure if the people in the beer garden have heard the news, so I venture outside to find Dicky. They obviously heard the announcement because they are all singing along too and jumping up and down. My stomach drops as I see Dicky hugging Kathy. Fucking great!

Once we've cleared up and the band has gone, I ask Jess if she'll clear up in the garden.

'I'm going to go upstairs to make sure it's nice and tidy for Jackson and Tammy to come home to. I really don't want to see Dicky with Kathy again either, if I'm being honest.'

'Don't be daft! If I was you, I'd take my sexy ass out there and give Dicky a lingering snog right in front of Kathy.'

'I know you would Jess.'

Whether the old flame has reignited or not, I can't stand to see them together. I really like her. I felt we were on the verge of something special. Something new and exciting. If she isn't over Kathy, I don't want to be a casual fling. I want a love affair with all the bells and whistles. I want romance, and I definitely do not want to be anybody's fuck buddy. I feel let down, and to be honest, a bit of a fool.

I busy myself by filling the dishwasher, plumping pillows and cushions, closing the curtains, straightening the bed, and spraying some air freshener around.

Jess makes me jump, as I hadn't heard her come up the stairs or enter the room. 'Dicky was asking where you were, so I told her you had gone home with a headache. Did I do the right thing?'

'Yes, yes, you did thanks, Jess'

'Listen, I honestly don't think she will go down that road again, Jo. Too much water under the bridge, and Dicky left her, not the other way round. Any unfinished business between them has nothing to do with lust or love on Dicky's part, in my opinion.'

'They looked pretty cosy when I went outside earlier,' I sulk.

'Well, Kathy might want Dicky, but I'm fairly certain that Dicky does not want Kathy.'

'Fairly certain?' This makes me feel worse.

'Okay, definitely certain! Stop worrying, I bet Kathy will be gone tomorrow. Don't forget, Kathy lived here for quite a while, so she would be pleased for Jackson and Tammy as well. You could go round Dicky's if you're that concerned?'

'No! I would look like a right loon. I have no claim on her, Jess. One night together does not make us girlfriends, or partners, or whatever. I just can't help feeling a bit pissed off.'

'Do you wanna come to mine, and we'll get shit faced?' Her face lights up at the prospect.

'No thanks, not tonight, sorry. I'm knackered and just want to go to bed. I'll take a rain check though, if that's okay?'

'No problem at all, anytime,' she replies, then adds, 'I'm sure you're reading too much into the Dicky and Kathy thing. I'll say it again, I honestly, truly, do not think she would go there again. Kathy repeatedly cheated on her. Then she left, then she came back several times. I know Dicky is sort of friends with her now, but she wasn't to begin with. You really need to speak to her, you know. There is probably stuff she hasn't told you yet that might explain everything, Jo.'

Curiosity getting the better of me, so I say, 'Well, that sounds like you know things that I don't?' Unusually for Jess, she doesn't respond in a straightforward way, she just shakes her head and says, 'Stop stressing, and besides, I heard Dicky has met someone new.' She winks and squeezes my arm as she gets up to leave.

For the next few days, I try my best to avoid Dicky. I don't want her to see the green-eyed monster when she looks at me. I'm also hoping that Kathy will bugger off.

I don't go to the café for my morning coffee for a few days. Instead, I take a lidded coffee cup down to the beach to enjoy the view and the peace.

I half hope Dicky is surfing (alone), but she isn't here today and wasn't yesterday either.

I keep imagining her in bed with Kathy. This thought is torture. A seagull lands near my feet. He's been here both mornings, I've called him 'Sid'. It could, of course, have been two different seagulls, but I choose to believe it's the same one. He gives me a knowing look, as if sensing something is wrong.

'Do me a favour, Sid, fly up to Dicky's bedroom window, and see who is in there, will you?'

He flies off but goes in the wrong direction. 'Stupid bird brain.'

Just before I am due to open at lunchtime, Jackson brings Tammy and their gorgeous baby daughter home.

They have named her Willow, how beautiful is that? She's just as beautiful as her name too. I hold her little hand, and she curls her fingers around my index finger. I can't take my eyes off her. She's perfect, with a shock of dark hair, a little squashed nose, and the tiniest finger nails I have ever seen.

Jess and I fuss around, making tea, and giving Tammy gifts of flowers, a cute little lemon romper suit, a teddy, and a beautiful handmade baby blanket that is so soft, it makes you want to stroke your face with it whenever you touch it.

Tammy and Jackson look tired, but happy. We leave them to enjoy their first day home with their baby, making Jackson promise not to come into work today and to call if they need anything.

To Jess' glee, Richard comes into the bar. Jess almost knocks me on my arse to get past me to serve him.

'What can I get you, handsome?' She really has got more confidence than anyone I know. I wouldn't have thought that Jess would be Richard's type somehow, or vice versa, but he gives Jess a little smirk. 'I'll have a pint of your finest please, Jessica, and a quick word with Jackson if he's around?'

'He has just brought Tammy home with the new baby, so he isn't available at the moment, I'm afraid. Is there anything I can help you with?' Jess has a cheeky grin on her face and has ramped up the flirting with a little lean on the bar, treating Richard to an eyeful of her cleavage.

'It's alright Jess.' Jackson walks into the bar. 'I'll take it from here.' He doesn't sound too friendly.

'I wanted to give you this.' Richard has a bag in his

hand and passes it over the bar to Jackson. 'It's the tankard some of the old boys in the village bought for my dad on his sixtieth birthday. Over twenty years ago now. I know it was before your time, Jackson, but I'm having a clear out and couldn't think of anywhere more fitting for this to go. I'd like to buy you a pint to put in it, to wet the baby's head, if you'll allow me?'

'That's very decent of you, Richard, and yes, I'll have a drink with you. Thank you. You're having a clear out to sell the farm then, I take it?' Jackson pulls them both a pint.

'I am, yes. I have no choice in it, Jackson.' Richard holds his pint up. 'To the new baby.' He takes a long swallow.

'Thank you.' Jackson does the same.

'Clearing the old place out is harder than I ever thought it would be. I know you all think of me as a heartless bastard, but the truth is, my business is in trouble. I've been offered a lot of money for that farm and the land it stands on. I'll go under if I don't sell. I'm no farmer, you know that. I wouldn't have a clue how to make a living.'

'Aye, I know, it's a tough one, I'll give you that.'

'I would prefer to sell to someone who would keep it as a farm, but no one has even put in an offer, so that's not going to happen. That old farmhouse needs knocking down and rebuilding for starters. I am sorry, you know.' His handsome face looks genuinely sad.

Jackson softens a little. 'Aye, I'm sure you are lad, and so will the majority in this village when them developers move in. Anyhow, it is what it is.'

'I best make a move. You wouldn't believe how much

stuff the old man collected over the years.' He rolls his eyes. 'Anyway, the best of health and happiness to all of you.'

Jackson raises his new tankard and says, 'Right back at you, Richard.' He then finishes his pint and makes his excuses to go back upstairs to Tammy and the baby.

Richard puts his unfinished pint on the bar and gives a sad smile to Jess and says, 'See you, Jess.'

'See you, Richard, don't be a stranger.' She smiles a sad smile. I think she really likes this one.

CHAPTER 13
GOODBYE MY FRIEND –
LINDA RONSTADT

I love my morning walk along the beach, which I finish off with a good quality coffee. Taking one to the beach that I've made myself just isn't the same. It's a small village, so it's not really possible to avoid anyone for long anyway. So, I'm going to the café for my coffee, and hopefully, I'll be able to find out if Dicky is with Kathy or not.

This morning, when I enter the café, it's busy for the time of day. It has started to rain, so the early morning walkers are probably sheltering for a while.

Young Sophie (as she's called in the village) is behind the counter, and she takes my order of coffee and a warm croissant. Margot walks in from the kitchen with her bright smile. 'Hello, darling! We've not seen you in a little while. How are you keeping?'

'I'm good, thank you, Margot. How are you?' I can't help but feel disappointed that Dicky isn't here, but everyone is entitled to a day off, I suppose.

'Oh, I'm marvellous, darling, or at least I will be once

Dicky is back from her little jaunt. Stella and I are planning a nice little break in the south of France. We try to get there every year, and there are two gentlemen eagerly awaiting our arrival.' She flashes me a suggestive smile and I reply, 'Good for you two.'

I can't help but ask because it's killing me, 'Dicky gone on holiday then, has she?'

'Not exactly, darling, she has gone to Kent to see Kathy. I'm sure she has filled you in about her. Anyway, I think she will be back in a day or so.'

I sit at the window, and although the rain has stopped and the clouds are blowing over, the view doesn't look quite so stunning this morning, the colours not so bright. I know I saw her hugging Kathy, but I had honestly hoped it was an innocent, platonic thing. You know, a 'see you when I see you' kinda hug. That hope is gone now. It appears Jess was wrong, and Dicky is interested in getting back with her ex after all, or at least interested enough to send her off to Kent. I wonder if she's going to bring her back. God, I hope not.

CHAPTER 14
CAN'T FEEL MY FACE –
THE WEEKND

I relay all this to Jess. 'Ring or text her, will you?' she says in an exasperated way.

'No, Jess, I'm not chasing after someone who doesn't want to be chased.'

'I don't think that is the case, Jo. I wouldn't say it if I thought that, honestly. You're not going to up sticks and fuck off back to wherever you came from, are you?'

I let out a sad laugh. 'Not if I can get another job, so I can pay my bills. I love it here, and I'll love it here regardless of Dicky. Even if Dicky brings Kathy back, I'll love it, probably just not as much.'

'Thank God for that. I love you being here. Something will turn up on the job front, I know it will.' She sits, biting her lip, and I assume she's thinking about a job for me.

'I tell you what, why don't I ask Jackson if you can have the night off, and we can sod off somewhere?' She looks at me hopefully.

I hesitate, thinking about how much it'll cost, but

sod it. 'Okay, yes, why not? If he can get some cover, that is. It'll do us good and stop me moping around.'

'Stay there, do not move!' She runs upstairs to Jackson. I'm guessing it's a no, but when she comes back down with a big, beaming smile, I know she has been successful. 'I take it that's a yes, then? You were gone ages, so I thought he had said no?'

'He had to do some ringing around, didn't he? Now go and pack an overnight bag, baby! I'll be at your cottage in half an hour!'

'Where are we going?' I feel much better at the thought of getting away from the village. Plus, Jess is such good fun. How can anyone be upset for long around her?

'Brighton! We'll have a good old-fashioned girls' night out.' She runs out of the door to go and pack a bag.

I don't know what to pack, so I pack something for every eventuality, and it might get cold tonight. Jess shouts me from the hallway, and I struggle to lug my bag downstairs.

She looks at me with one hand on her hip. I notice she has a tiny little bag. I drop my bag on the floor with a heavy thud. Jess unzips it and throws out most of the contents.

"It's fucking eighty degrees in the shade. What you got jumpers in here for? And jeans and trainers? No, no, no. You just need one outfit for tonight, clean knickers, and maybe a clean t-shirt for fuck's sake. You can take your makeup, toiletries and a towel.'

'Won't the hotel have towels?' She couldn't have heard me because she doesn't answer.

When I look at what is left, I realise I don't need my holdall. It would all fit quite easily into my handbag.

'Okay, okay,' I say, looking at the big pile of clothes on the floor. 'Let's go! Have you booked us into a hotel or B&B, Jess?'

'Kind of,' she says, throwing our bags into my boot.

We get inside the car, and I pull away from the curb. 'Oh god, what do you mean, kind of?' I suddenly feel dread creeping in.

'Well, it's the YMCA, as we're on a budget. I decided to save on accommodation, so we have more money for drinks and stuff. But you'll be happy to know it's a female-only dorm!' She smiles like she's just told me we have a room with a hot tub on the balcony and our own personal butler.

I concentrate on the road, as I do not know what to say. What I want to say is, 'A fucking dorm! Are you kidding me?' Instead, I just breathe through my panic. I honestly cannot think of anything worse than sharing a room with a load of strangers, female only or otherwise. It's a goddamn nightmare!

She clearly has no clue of my inner anger because she turns the radio up full blast and sings 'Woah, I'm going to Ibiza' at full pelt.

I don't want to spoil it by sulking, so I sing along and before long, I find myself loosening up and enjoying the journey.

Parking at hotels in Brighton is virtually obsolete, and the whole thing is a bit of a nightmare, so we find a car park first, then walk to the YMCA.

'Bet you're glad you didn't bring all that stuff now,

aren't you?' she says happily, swinging her little bag over her shoulder.

'Mm.'

The dorm is massive, but basic, to say the least. There are eight beds in here and a row of lockers with keys. I guess this is so that your shower gel doesn't go missing. We bagsy some bunk beds near the window. I very quickly sit on the bottom bunk, letting Jess know which one is mine. All the beds have folded bedding on them (you have to make them up yourself), so we do this first. This way, when other people come in, they'll know these two are ours. We put our clothes and toiletries in a locker, put a pound in the slot, and lock them.

'Fancy a liquid lunch?' Jess asks, rubbing her hands together very excitedly and is clearly much happier with our sleeping arrangements than I am. But I really am trying hard not to show that I could strangle her. If we ever do this again, I am booking the room! I'm not a snob, but I thought we would have a little room with twin beds and an en-suite bathroom!

'I'd like a food-based lunch, to be honest, Jess. I'm starving, and if I drink on an empty stomach, I'll be back in my bunk before dinner time.'

She tuts, and we head out to find a pub that does food. It's quite busy already and by the time our food arrives, I've almost finished a large glass of wine, and Jess is on her second.

It's a beautiful day, so after we lunch, I ask Jess if she wants to sit on the beach for a while. It's not a sandy beach, more pebbles, but it's still lovely.

'Haven't you been away with any mates before, Jo?' She looks really puzzled.

'Erm, I went on some day trips with some friends from uni a few times. Why?'

'Well two things, for a start, we have a much nicer beach at home that you can sit on without getting a rock up your arse, and secondly, we haven't come here to sit on the bloody beach and take in the scenery! We've come to get rat arsed, practise your flirting, and have a laugh!'

'Okay, gotcha.'

We find a bar with a terrace on the roof and sit there all afternoon, drinking. It's fun actually. Jess talks to literally everybody and flirts unashamedly with males and females alike.

I see two girls kissing at a nearby table, and I can't help but think of Dicky. Why does everything have to be so complicated? I can't believe I have fallen for a woman. A few months ago, I would've laughed and said, 'It's just not me!' But I am slowly coming to the realisation that it is me. Oh well, c'est la vie and all that.

Jess talks to two women, Tasha and Bee. She firstly finds out that they are just friends, then that they are lesbians. Honestly, I could strangle her. As Jess is chatting away to Tasha, I have no option but to engage Bee in conversation. She is funny and I find myself enjoying her company. We have quite a few drinks and shots, and I get very giggly. I'm not romantically interested in her, in the least, but I'm having fun, and I guess that's the point of this trip.

To my surprise, it's Jess that suggests we go back to the room to shower and change.

As we approach our room, I hear music and talking, and for a second, I wonder who the hell has broken into our room. Then, I remember that we're in a shared room, for God's sake.

There are four other youngish women, clearly getting ready for a night out and at different stages of undress. Two of them are the spitting image of each other, and I can't decide if they are twins or sisters. Same blonde hair, same height and slim body shape. The other two, who are singing loudly, look nothing like each other. One is much shorter and curvier than the other, but both of them have a good pair of lungs on them.

'Hello ladies!' shouts Jess above the music. 'I'm Jess, and this is Jo.' They each have a glass filled with some sort of psychedelic liquid. One of them grabs two more plastic glasses and pours us one.

I sniff it warily as Jess puts her finger under my glass and gently guides it to my lips while pouring hers down her throat in one continuous movement.

I am forced to drink several more of this toxic substance, and to be honest, I feel great!

We shower (sort of) and apply fresh make-up. I think I've just applied a new coat over the old, but I couldn't be sure or care less at this point.

One of the girls asks if we want to go out with them to see a drag act. I'm about to turn them down when Jess jumps in. 'Fantastic! Course we do, eh, Jo?'

'Erm, yes, of course we do.' I try to make it sound more enthusiastic than I feel.

All the other girls are dressed in skimpy bright outfits. There sure is a lot of body confidence in this room! I have nothing like that in my little bag (thankfully).

I have on my trusty denim skirt, which is short enough for me, and a plain black t-shirt.

Jess takes one look at me and shakes her head. 'The skirt is fine, but that t-shirt isn't very sexy, is it? Let's see what we can do with you.'

'You chucked all my clothes out of my bag, Jess remember? I have nothing else to wear.'

'Anyone got any scissors?' she shouts.

Oh god, what the actual fuck?

She manages to get some nail scissors. Who the hell gave her those? And she promptly sets herself to work, wrecking my t-shirt!

First, she chops five inches off the bottom, cuts off the little sleeves, then (and this is the part where I desperately want to stop her artistic flare), she cuts slits all over it, making sure there's plenty of *everything* on show. Great, I look like I've been in a cat fight with a tiger! Oh well, no choice but to brazen it out.

The drag queens look fabulous in the biggest, brightest dresses and wigs I've ever seen.

The club has big round tables with a lamp in the centre of each, giving it an old-fashioned look. Our table is at the front, so we have a perfect view of the stage. The atmosphere is buzzing and everyone is dancing in their seats and singing along.

One of the drag queens calls herself 'Tina Head-Turner'. This set is all Tina Turner tracks with the moves and all.

She asks for some backing dancers, and Jess jumps up, dragging me (literally dragging me) onto the stage!

She gives us some moves, which she expects us to perform as she lip syncs to 'Proud Mary'.

I have never been more out of my comfort zone in my life. Jess is doing a good impression of High School Musical meets Diversity, whilst I look like the living dead.

However, the audience are clearly loving it as they are all on their feet, clapping and singing along. This gives me some much needed confidence, and I feel myself loosening up and giving it big licks. By the end of the song, I'm doing a good impression of Michael Flatley on whiz.

Bolstered up with my newfound confidence, we head to a few more bars, and I even get up with Jess on karaoke to sing 'Girls Just Wanna Have Fun!' Badly, I must admit.

Jess tries to get me to flirt with a few girls, but I decline and tell her I am having a good time just as we are. This does not stop Jess, though. I return from the loo to find her snogging the face off some random girl. So much for experiencing being a lesbian vicariously through me.

I am so drunk it feels like the floor is moving, and I can't feel my legs. Oh God, I can't feel my face! Time for bed, I think.

Jess is up bright-eyed and bushy-tailed the following morning, showing no signs of a hangover. She insists we have a big breakfast before heading back home.

I can just about manage some coffee and toast whilst she tucks into a full English breakfast, which she says isn't complete without black pudding. Gross.

Once I've dropped Jess off at home, the first thing I

do is fall face down on my bed and have a little sleep. Three hours later, I wake with a start, fearing that I'm late for work, then I remember I'm not working until tomorrow.

I do some work in my garden, walk on the beach, and before I know it, it's seven o'clock, and I'm starving. I go into the Stern for a chicken wrap, and Jess is behind the bar.

'I've been up to the farm this afternoon,' she says. 'I thought I would go and see if Richard needed another pair of hands to help sort his dad's stuff out, horrible job on your own.'

'And?' She's giving nothing away with her facial expression.

'Well, there's good news and bad news. The good news is that he said he has had someone put in an offer for the farm that wants to keep it as a farm. But the bad news is it's not as much money as the hotel development has offered.'

'Oh right, well, that's that then.'

'I don't know, you know. He is torn, but he needs the money for his business. Although, he did say that he doesn't know why he bothers. He was saying how much stress he's under all the time and how he works such long hours. Oh yeah, and he asked if I wanted to go out for dinner with him, but I said no because I'm working tonight.' She kind of snuck that little nugget of information in at the end.

'Why did you say no? I thought you really liked him!'

'I do, I really do actually, but what would be the point? I would go out with him, get to like him even more, then he'd sod off miles away, and he would never

126

come back. I'm not doing that to myself. I do have feel-
ings too, you know.' She looks a bit fed up for a second,
then her face brightens. 'He said I'm lovely, and he
cannot believe it has only just dawned on him. I'd be
buzzing if he was sticking around.'

'Ah, Jess, that's a real bummer.' I pat her hand, as I do
feel sorry for her. 'There really is a lack of eligible bache-
lors in this village, isn't there?'

'No shit! We need to go out to town more, don't we?'

'Yes, we could do, or have you tried any dating sites?'

'Yes, I have and just for the record, never again!' She
is shaking her head quite emphatically.

'Go on, what happened?' I can't help but smile,
wondering what's coming.

'Well, for a start, I've been catfished on more than
one occasion. When one guy showed up at the restau-
rant, I thought he had sent his dad to tell me he was
going to be late or something. It turns out he was my
bloody date!' She laughs, shaking her head at the
memory.

'What did you do? Did you make an excuse and
leave?'

'No, did I heck. I stayed and had a meal with him, I
felt a bit sorry for him.'

I laugh. 'You're such a softy.'

'Tell me about it. I had to listen to him bang on
about his late wife! For two and a half hours! I thought
Keith was an old name for someone supposedly in their
twenties.' She puts her face in her hands to quell the
giggles, which starts me off, and it's several minutes
before we pull ourselves together. 'So, online dating is
not something I will be trying again in a hurry.'

'No, I can see why.'

Back at my cottage, I take a cup of tea into my garden and sit to watch dusk turn into night.

I feel happy and sad at the same time. Happy with all this, this garden feels like my little haven, but a little sad that what I hoped to be a steamy love affair turned into nothing but a one-night stand.

Just as I am thinking about this, there's a knock on my front door. I only just hear it, as I'm deep in thought and feeling a little dozy.

I open the door to find Dicky standing with her hands in the pockets of her jeans.

'Hello,' she says, 'I'm back.'

'So I see, erm, do you want to come in?'

'No, I just thought I'd knock on your door for the fun of it.' She smiles, and I stand to one side to let her pass.

Walking into the kitchen, I pour us both a glass of wine without asking if she wants one. I figure this conversation might be better with wine instead of tea. I lead the way outside into the garden. Once we are seated, she says, 'The garden is looking lovely, you wouldn't recognise it now, must've taken hours.'

'Yes, it has.' I sigh. 'You're back from visiting Kathy then?'

'Yes, I'm sure Jess filled you in on the whole story,' she says this as a statement rather than a question.

'I don't know if she has or not. She only mentioned that Kathy was your ex. She said your relationship with her ended badly, but that's about it.' I'm fiddling with the stem of my wine glass, waiting for her to say she's moving out of the village, and I realise how heavy my heart feels.

Dicky sighs. 'Well, there's a bit more to it than just that.'

'I figured there must be.' I interrupt her.

She waits a beat, then carries on. 'We were together for a long time, and almost got married at one point. Anyway, we lived together, shared everything, and I thought we were happy. Kathy had a little girl. I didn't know she had cheated on me until she was too far along to hide it. She didn't know who the father was, or so she said, as she had a one tressy on a trip to see her folks. Anyway, once the shock of the pregnancy, and the heart-break of her cheating, had worn off a bit, we decided to raise the baby together. We played equal roles in her life.'

'Is that the little girl in the photos in your flat? How old is she? What's her name?'

'Yes, gorgeous, isn't she?' She takes a deep breath. 'Meadow, and she turned three two days ago. That's why I went to see her. You see, Kathy hasn't been letting me see her. I got back with Kathy several times because that was the only way I could see Meadow and spend time with her. I should've adopted her when we were together, but I didn't. I'm not listed on any paperwork either, and of course, we aren't married or in a civil part-nership, so it makes it more complicated to fight for access. Not impossible, though.'

'So, are you going back to Kathy, then?'

Dicky gives a mirthless laugh. 'No, I couldn't go there again. She made my life hell for a long time. I love that little girl though, and she loves me. She calls me

Mummy, and that's how I see her, as my daughter. We shared her care, so the bond between us was, and still is, as strong as any blood relative's. No, I went to see Meadow and talk to Kathy about regular access. I said I'm prepared to go to court, but thank God, she has finally agreed to let me have her for one weekend a month.' She beams, and my heart goes out to her.

'What if she goes back on it? Don't you need a solicitor to do an agreement or something?'

'Maybe, but it wouldn't be worth shit if she decided to change her mind. Anyway, it probably won't come to that, as there are two things going in my favour. She has a new woman in her life, so she is glad to be child free once a month. And, when I got there, she saw the absolute joy on Meadow's face. She said she felt bad for keeping us apart for so long.' She takes a drink of wine, and suddenly looks tired.

'I can't believe you didn't tell me all of this before. Jess kept telling me to speak to you, but I never guessed why.'

Dicky laughs. 'Hi, I'm Dicky, and I'm going through hell fighting for access to my ex's child because she is a cow. Something like that, you mean?'

'Well, obviously not, no, but we were getting pretty close, or I thought we were, so you could've mentioned her to me. Plus, you seemed to be okay with each other at the pub during the surfing competition, not that I was keeping tabs on you.' I feel embarrassed that she might think I was watching her the whole time.

'We spent most of the time talking about Meadow, and I was trying to persuade her to let me be a part of her life, and it appears I succeeded! That's why I have come to see you tonight. To share, what is for me, excellent news, and to see you, of course. I'm shocked Jess didn't tell you about Meadow. I thought she would've. Then, when you didn't text, I thought having a small child in the mix had put you off me.'

'Jess obviously thought it was something you had to tell me yourself and not her news to share.' I smile, and she smiles back, and this time, it reaches her eyes and feels genuine.

'And is having a small child in the mix off-putting for you?' This is obviously a deal breaker, so I need to tread carefully, but I should be honest at the same time.

'To be honest, I've never wanted kids of my own. I don't think I'm grown up enough to look after a child.' I laugh, but Dicky doesn't. She just smiles slightly.

'So, you're saying you don't like them?' she asks, looking a little upset.

'No, not at all. I do like them. I've just not had a lot of dealings with kids as there aren't any in my family. I love little Willow, though, and I think she likes me too, well she doesn't cry when I cuddle her. Perhaps Meadow will like me as well, if I get to meet her.' I look at her hopefully.

'Yes, maybe she will.' She seems to have been placated, so I change the subject.

I tell her about the night in Brighton, and she laughs through my stories. In particular, Jess cutting my t-shirt until it was virtually non-existent. I miss out some of the night's antics, of course.

I fill her in about Jess being asked out for dinner by Richard and how Jess declined his offer, even though she really likes him, and from what I can tell, he likes her too.

Dicky agrees that we need to go out into town, so Jess has a better chance of meeting someone.

Dicky gets up to go, so I walk her to the door. My heart is hammering, thinking of another kiss from her, but when we get to the door, I don't think a kiss is on her mind tonight because she hesitates. I take hold of her hand and gently pull her towards me. Her kiss is soft and slow and makes all of my senses tingle with desire.

'I'll see you tomorrow?' She pulls away and is looking into my eyes, hers crinkle a little at the sides in a smile.

'Absolutely you will. Goodnight.'

She raises her hand in a wave, and I sigh as she walks up the path.

CHAPTER 15

IT'S NOT OVER YET – FOR KING AND COUNTRY

The next morning is drizzly and grey, but now me and Dicky have sorted out our misunderstandings, I feel sunny and as happy as a pig in shit.

I am sipping my coffee and watching Dicky work when Stella comes in, and I indicate for her to sit with me.

'I was out for my morning walk earlier, and there are men with clipboards up on Wilf's cliff. I expect we will see some changes up there soon.' She shakes her head in disapproval.

'I didn't realise Richard had sold it already. I'd have thought Jess would've told me.' I realise by Stella's expression that I may have let a big fat cat out of the bag.

'She's been helping him pack up the farm, horrible job to do alone, you know what a softy she is,' I babble, trying to smooth over the fact that most people would see Jess as a traitor for helping Richard.

'It doesn't hurt that he's extremely handsome either,

I should imagine.' Stella smiles, and I smile back, feeling relieved. I should've known better than to assume Stella would be all judgey.

I say goodbye to Stella, wave to Dicky, and walk up there to have a look for myself. The drizzle has almost stopped, and even though it's not bright and sunny, the view from up here is still beautiful.

There are no developers up here now, so I sit down and take a look around at the fields that may not be here for much longer. It's lovely. I notice that there are only a few meadow clary flowers left, which is normal for this time of year. I suddenly remember having a lecture at uni about endangered plants, birds, and butterflies. Somewhere in the back of my brain, a little bell starts ringing. I feel almost certain that the meadow clary was mentioned in a lecture about endangered plant species. Oh my God, if I am right, we could throw a spanner in the works. Maybe even save the clifftop. A long shot, but stranger things have happened. I have some checking to do, before I get ahead of myself.

I do some research on Meadow Clary on my phone. It is indeed endangered. My heart skips a beat, and I virtually run down from the cliff, almost falling arse over tit in the process. I put a call through to my old university and ask to speak to my old tutor, Dave Preston, who taught us about endangered plants. He isn't available, so I leave a message for him to call me back as soon as he can, then I email him some photos of the plant. I just need to wait to see what he comes back with. I have everything crossed.

After our lunchtime shift, Jess insists we drive into town to get a coffee.

'Why did you want to come here and not go to Dicky's café?' It doesn't make any sense to me why we'd drive out here when we have a perfectly lovely café with a perfectly lovely owner within walking distance.

'I thought a change would do us good,' she replies.

I squint at her, not convinced.

'Okay, I wanted to talk to you away from the village ears.' She fiddles with her coffee cup.

'Now, I'm interested. What's up?' I shuffle in my seat to get comfy.

'It's Richard.' She looks into her coffee with a frown.

'Handsome but not very nice Richard? Selling the farm to developers Richard?'

'Yes. I mean no, he is nice, Jo. He's really nice, in actual fact. I really like him, and I think he really likes me. Anyway, I've been helping him box all the stuff up, and we've gotten a bit close.' She gives a weak smile.

'Oh, how close?'

'Pretty close. Anyway, I don't want him to sell the farm. Plus, I don't think he really wants to. I suggested he doesn't sell, but he just said he knows nothing about farming. He's never got involved in it, never had any interest in farming.' She looks close to tears, and my heart goes out to her.

I want to ask her more about the 'pretty close' part, but now clearly isn't the time.

'Can't you still see him if he doesn't live in the bay? Other people date who don't live within spitting distance of each other. What is it, a two hour drive, if that?'

'Yes, I know, but he runs a company that takes up all of his time. He works super long hours and even week-ends a lot of the time.' She looks so miserable, so I rub her arm, not really knowing what to say.

'What does he do, anyway?' I ask.

'Dunno.' She gives a sad little laugh. 'Something in computers or whatever. He did tell me when I asked him, but I didn't really understand what he was going on about.' She wipes her face with both hands, then continues, 'He knows my background, that I wasn't always the upstanding citizen that I am now, but he doesn't care. I don't have to hide anything from him. That's unusual, isn't it?'

I nod and say, 'Ah, I don't have any answers, Jess, no words of wisdom that'll make you feel better.'

'I didn't think you would. I just wanted to talk to you about it. No one in the village likes him much, so I've been keeping it to myself, and it's horrible.' She sniffs again and wipes her nose on a serviette.

'You can tell me anything, you know that.' I really want to tell Jess about the Meadow Clary and how that might delay things, but I don't want to get her hopes up, just in case I'm wrong.

A few days later, I receive a call from Dave Preston, at the uni. He has studied the pictures of the flowers I emailed him, and he agrees that they are indeed Meadow Clary. We talk about it for an hour, and I make notes as he speaks so that I don't forget anything. He said the flowers probably won't stop any development, but legal wrangling could delay things considerably. I'm bursting to tell the others the news, so as soon as I put the phone down, I run to the Stern. It's chucking it down with rain, and as I run, I splash through puddles, not caring one bit.

Jess, Jackson, and Tammy are all gathered around our usual pre-work table in the pub with a cup of tea. Tammy has Willow over her shoulder and is rubbing her back.

'I have some news!' I announce as I burst through the door, bumping into Willow's pram, looking like a drowned rat, making them all jump and making Willow stir, who thankfully, is not in her pram.

'Crikey, petal, what's on fire?' Jackson stands and looks a bit worried.

'Sorry, sorry, Tammy, nothing is wrong. In fact, it may be good. The thing is, Meadow Clary, Salvia Pratensis, to be exact, you know, the flowers that grow up on the cliff, are threatened and are specifically protected under the 1992 amendment to schedule 8 of the Wildlife and Countryside Act 1981. It is an offence to pick, uproot, or damage any plants listed on the Schedule 8 status. Moreover, butterflies and bees love it. One such butterfly is the high brown fritillary, whose caterpillar eats it and is also endangered!'

They all sit looking at me blankly. Jess says, '"Moreover?" Who the fuck says "moreover?"'

'That's what you focus on from what I've just said, Jess?' I hold my palms face up in a questioning fashion.

'Okay, lass, what does this mean exactly?' Jackson says, ignoring Jess's sarcasm.

'What it means is that we have a couple of spanners to throw into the works! We can, at best, stop the development, but from what I have learnt today from my old uni tutor, it's more likely that we can delay it by a considerable amount of time, could be months.'

'Time that Richard doesn't have.' Jess throws in, biting her lip.

'Exactly, Jess, if he can't sell it straight away, he'll most likely lose his business, anyway. So, he might stay.' I pick up a hobnob from the plate in the middle of the table and bite into it.

'Anyway, Dave, knows far more about it than I do, so he has advised me what to do next. In the meantime, I need to tell Richard to stop whatever they are planning for the time being.' I look at Jess, who doesn't look as happy as I thought this news would make her.

'Jess? You okay?'

'Erm, yes, I'll speak to Richard, if that's okay with you?'

'Of course, but why the long face? This could mean Richard stays here, Jess!'

'I know, but I want him to want to stay, not to be forced into staying.' She takes her phone from her back pocket.

'Okay, but don't you think this is a conversation you should have face to face? I don't think it's news you should share over the phone, Jess.'

'Obviously, I'm just going to ask him whether he's at the farm or if he's gone back already.' I thought she would be happier than she is.

Jess leaves the room to call Richard, and Jackson says, 'Well done, Jo! How did you know about that flower? Let's have a little drink to celebrate.' He stands and goes behind the bar.

'I studied botany, so plants are sort of my thing,' I tell him.

'No alcohol for me, love,' Tammy says, 'I don't want Willow getting tipsy. I'm going to take her for a walk, but you all go ahead.' She says, tucking Willow into her pram.

Coming back in through the doorway, Jess says, 'Nor for me either, Jackson, I'm going up to the farm to see Richard before he shoots off. I'll have one when I come back. I'll probably need it.' She heads out of the door, raising her hand to us.

'Let's save it until later then, shall we, Jackson? When we can all have one, eh?'

'Aye, okay, pet, I've got a list of jobs to do, anyway. But thank you, and well done. This village won't be able to thank you enough if this stops the development. And if it doesn't, the fact that you've tried will mean a lot to us all. So don't go worrying if it doesn't go the way we hope, okay?" He gives me one of his bear hugs and heads into the cellar.

'Right, Mum, a little bit of magic would be good,' I whisper.

CHAPTER 16
TENNESSEE WHISKEY – CHRIS STAPLETON

I text Dicky, asking if she would like to come to my cottage tonight, as I have something to tell her. She replies within minutes to accept. She'll be with me around seven. I can't wait to tell her the news.

Jess has been gone for ages, and I'm dying for her to come back so that she can tell us what Richard's reaction was. I'm starting to get worried, as I have texted her asking if she is okay, and she just texted back, *Fine*.

I find myself pacing up and down, worried that Richard might have kicked off. So I send a text saying, *More information needed, what does fine mean?* I get another vague text from Jess saying, *Don't worry, I'll see you tomorrow*.

For goodness' sake, I hate suspense. I can't even watch a suspense movie unless it's from behind a cushion!

I busy myself making the cottage look lovely, no clothes lying around, clean sheets, smells nice, candle lit, and top it off by opening a bottle of red to breathe.

I have an hour until Dicky gets here. The cottage looks nice, so I need to make myself look presentable too. I'm just getting ready to jump in the shower when I hear a knock on the door. I throw on my little dressing gown and run downstairs. Whoever it is needs to bugger off quick.

It's Dicky! Shit, she's early!

'Hi, sorry I'm early, but I was just waiting around, so I thought I would head over to drop this off.' She is holding a bag and hands it over. 'I'll come back in an hour if you're busy? She looks me up and down and has a sexy glint in her eye.

'You don't need to bring gifts every time you come round, you know. And no, don't be daft. You don't need to go. Come in and pour yourself a glass of wine. I just need to have a quick shower.' She raises one eyebrow and my heart starts hammering. Oh God, she has a very profound effect on me, in a good way.

'I've got a better idea. Why don't I keep you company?'

My whole body tingles and shakes with anticipation, and I just stand in silence for a second, then I think fuck it, and I take her hand and lead her upstairs to the bathroom.

Dicky gets her phone out of her pocket and puts on some music. 'What's this? I love it.'

'Tennessee Whiskey, I'm glad you like it.' She stands in front of me and slowly starts to undo her shirt, keeping eye contact with me the whole time. I'm unsure whether to help or not, but I'm enjoying the show, so I sit on the closed lid of the toilet.

She removes her boots, then jeans, and is standing in

just her underwear. I stand in front of her, and she bites her bottom lip while she slips my dressing gown from my shoulders. I undo her bra, releasing her full breasts. I reach out to touch her, but she moves away slightly. She then removes her pants so that we are standing naked in front of each other.

As I lean around her to turn on the shower, her breast strokes my cheek. We step inside and explode in a passionate kiss. I can taste her minty breath, smell her intoxicating smell, hear her breathing getting heavier, and feel her lovely, smooth body pressed against mine. She stops and pours shower gel down my front. She rubs it into my breasts, stomach, arms, and I can hardly stand it. Despite the warm water, I have goosebumps all over. It feels so good. She turns me around so that I have my back to her and works her magic on every inch of my body, stroking, rubbing, kissing my neck, and gently tugging on my hair. She takes the shower off its cradle and rinses my body before kneeling down in front of me. Oh my God, this is definitely one of those times that, no matter what, you can't come quietly.

Stepping out of the shower, I take her hand, and we go through to the bedroom without drying off. I quickly close the window, push her onto the bed, and lean over her on all fours. She moans with pleasure when I let my wet hair trail down her body. I lick and suck her nipples, then I let my tongue follow the water trail down her torso. She is so ready, but I stop to let her come back down for a second or two. I hear her say, 'Bastard' under her breath, and I give her a mischievous smile. She pushes my head down, and it's a mere minute until she reaches a loud orgasm.

We both lie next to each other in bed, panting and satisfied. 'Thank God you closed the window.' She chuckles.

We start to get chilly, so we dress and go downstairs.

'Anyway, what did you have to tell me?'

'Well, long story short, the flower on the clifftop is Meadow Clary, and it's endangered. So, hopefully, there will be a delay in the development.'

'Meaning what?'

'Hang on, that's what I'm telling you. Meaning, that if it doesn't sell now, Richard might not sell at all. Jess has gone to talk to him, and it's driving me nuts because she's been gone ages!'

Before I can say any more, there's another knock on the front door.

'Hi, Jess, come in,' I say, feeling relieved that she wasn't half an hour earlier.

When she steps into the lounge, she's panting, as if she's been running. She stops short and says, 'Oh, hi, Dicky. Sorry, I didn't know you were here. I won't stay. I will see you later. No worries.' She turns to leave, but I stop her.

'No, you don't. Sit down. I'll get you a glass of wine.'

'I don't want to interrupt anything,' she says this as a question, then says, 'I know I said I would come see you tomorrow, but I thought I would put you out of your misery. Although, from the look of the pair of you, there isn't much misery to put you out of.'

'Nope, your timing is perfect.' Dicky shoots me a look, then goes to get Jess some wine.

'So?' I ask before she has even had the chance to sit down.

'Well, you won't need to be getting any wildlife trust or whatever involved to stop the development, Jo.' She gets up from the chair and sits next to me on the settee.

Dicky brings the wine in and, as she's handing it to her, says, 'And?'

'I can't quite believe it. We talked for hours, well most of the time we were talking.' She wiggles her eyebrows, which makes us both laugh. 'Anyway, I told Richard about the flowers and stuff. I'm not sure if I said it how you said it, but he got the gist of it. I told him that there would be a significant delay. I thought he would be angry or disappointed, but he wasn't, well if he was, he didn't show it. He just went quiet and thoughtful for a while. I waited for him to speak, but I got fed up of waiting. So, I told him about my ideas. You see, I've been working on some ideas, well fantasising really. I didn't expect him to go for it in a thousand years. But he likes them, well loves them actually, and he wants to give them a try. He said he was having major second thoughts about selling anyway! He said he doesn't want to leave me behind!' she shouts the last part and does this little jiggly thing.

'You moving in with Richard, then?' I'm worried that it's all a bit quick.

'Don't be a twat, Jo, course I'm not. Well, not until I know it's the right thing for us both, and he hasn't asked me, and if he had, I'd have said no—'

Dicky interrupts her, 'Okay, start again, I have no idea what you're talking about.' She looks at me and asks, 'Have you, Jo?'

I shrug and shake my head. 'What ideas? You haven't said anything to me about any ideas.'

'Just some ideas about what Richard could do with the farm if he didn't want to keep it as a farm.' She looks between me and Dicky.

'Thanks for sharing that, Jess. I still have no idea what's going on, so I'll just go and top us up.' Dicky gets up and picks up our glasses.

'Not for me, thanks, Dicky, I've gotta go.' Jess puts her hand over her almost empty glass.

'Are you going to tell us exactly what he's going to give a go or not?' She's getting on my nerves now, beating around the bush.

'If you don't mind, I need to speak to Jackson and Tammy as well. So how about we all meet in the pub tomorrow before lunch, and I'll explain everything.'

'Okay, but it's going to kill me until then. I won't sleep!' I pull a mad face at her.

'Then find something to do to tire yourself out,' she says with a laugh, then she knocks what's left of her wine back and leaves us to it.

CHAPTER 17
GOOD NEWS – MANIC DRIVE

J ess, Tammy, and Jackson are seated at our usual table in the pub before opening, with a mug of tea each, and there's an extra one sitting waiting for me.

'Dicky sends her apologies, she's at the café on her own this morning. I'll fill her in later,' I say as I shimmy around Willow's empty pram and take my seat.

'What's all this about Jess?' Jackson is holding Willow, and his rocking motion is making me feel sea sick. I really must get out of the habit of drinking wine every night. But it's a lovely sight to see this big, tough man, being so gentle, holding his little baby.

Jess is jittery with excitement, and she can hardly contain it. 'I spoke to Richard yesterday and told him what Jo had told all of us, that there's likely to be a delay and all that stuff.'

Tammy's eyes go wide. 'Was he mad? What did he say?' Willow starts to cry, so she takes her from Jackson to feed her.

146

'No, he wasn't. He said he was relieved, and he was having second thoughts anyway, and he's okay about it not happening.' She picks up her tea and raises it in a cheers motion.

'Good grief, not what I expected you to say, pet.' Jackson puffs out his cheeks, and Tammy says, 'I thought he said he doesn't know anything about farming.'

'Hang on, there's more, a lot more, and it includes you two and this pub in a roundabout kinda way.' She takes a sip of tea, and we all wait for her to continue.

'Richard said to me a little while ago that he doesn't really like his city life or his job, for that matter. He said he hasn't really got a life outside of work, as the business takes up all his time and energy. He had to let his staff go, and he's been trying to keep things going single-handedly since. Anyway, he had an offer for his business ages ago, which he turned down, as he didn't want to sell it at the time. So, it's probably a long shot, but he's going to ask them if they still want to buy it. And if they don't, he said he'll just dissolve it. Life's not all about money.'

'That's a bit of a turnaround, isn't it?' Jackson still looks dubious.

'Yes, it is, but we've been getting to know each other a bit, you see.' Jess looks into her tea, as if not quite sure how Jackson will take this.

Tammy chuckles, and Jackson says, 'Jessica, my love, do you think we're daft or blind? Every spare minute you get, you can be seen running up that cliff path to the farm.' He pats her hand good-naturedly.

Jess clears her throat and visibly relaxes.

'I've been thinking over the last few weeks about what the farm, or more importantly, the farm buildings could be used for.' She pulls a well-used notepad from her bag. She flicks through the pages and stops somewhere in the middle. Blimey, she has been busy. There's notes, drawings and things crossed out on almost every page.

'He is going to convert the biggest barn, the one that has the view of the sea, into a wedding and conference venue! Imagine a wedding up on that cliff top!'

'It would be idyllic and so romantic.' Tammy looks at Jackson. 'We could renew our wedding vows, and you love a party.'

'Aye. So, Richard is going to go for this then, Jess?' Jackson looks at her, taking no notice of the comment from Tammy.

'Yes! He is. He loves it, and it will be good for all the businesses in the village. People will need accommodation. They'll shop here, come to eat and drink if they're staying a few days. What do you think? Do you love it?' Her excitement is visible and contagious.

'I do. This is the best news this village has had in ages. It's much better than having a hotel up there, that's for sure. Thanks to you two, it looks like it is all going to be a distant worry. Well done. I think we need Mrs Pete to call a village meeting so we can share the news. Ask Richard if he wants to announce it, Jess. And of course, we need a celebration! We haven't had a themed night for ages. What do you all think?' We all nod and he continues, 'We've not had a country and western night for a few years, that used to be quite popular.' He beams at us.

'Told you, didn't I? Any excuse for a party. I'm so pleased, well done, you two. Plus, I could do with a night off. Willow can go to my parents for the night, they've been dying to have her,' Tammy says as she puts a sleeping Willow into her pram.

Keiron, on his way to the kitchen, says, "Oh, country and western. "Brokeback Mountain" eat your heart out.' He fans his face with his hand.

Everyone is assembled for the village meeting at the Stern. There are people here I didn't even know who lived in the village.

Mrs Pete is trying to bring the place to order by tapping the table with her hand, but the excited chatter is louder than she is. A table has been placed in front of the fireplace, with only the Chairperson, Mrs Pete, sitting behind it. The rest of us are squashed around tables, and every available seat is occupied. Quite a few people are standing at the bar. Me, Dicky, and Jess have managed to bagsy a table near the back of the room.

'Okay, folks, can we have a bit of order, please?' Jackson booms above the noise, and it dies down enough for Mrs Pete to be heard.

'We are gathered here today—' she starts.

'You should've started that with, 'Dearly beloved!' shouts Jess. There's a brief rumble of laughter around the room before Mrs Pete continues. 'Thank you, Jessica.' She pauses. 'For those of you who haven't heard already, Jackson has some news that affects all of us.'

'Nay, it isn't my news, I think I'll let Joanna 'ere tell it, as she is the one that started it all. It's because of her that we have any news to tell.' Jackson nods at me and takes his place behind the bar.

I look around in shock. I wasn't expecting to have to speak. Dicky winks at me, and Jess shoves me in the shoulder and starts to clap. The whole place then claps along, and I feel my face burning bright red as I slowly stand up.

'Erm, well, as some of you may or may not know, the Meadow Clary flowers up on the clifftop are protected. I won't go into the ins-and-outs of it right now, but it means that the development could've been delayed too long to make it viable for the landowner, Richard to sell.'

Clapping and whistling ensues.

'Anyway, it turns out that Richard is happy with this and doesn't want to sell the farm after all. We were hoping he would be here tonight to tell you of his plans, but he sent his apologies as he couldn't make it. I will, however, leave this for Richard to tell you when he next comes in. All I will say is that this is good news for all of us. Thank you.' I need a drink!

'A glass of white wine, please, Jackson,' I say, walking up and leaning on the bar.

'This one is on the house, pet,' Jackson says, pouring a generous measure and handing me the glass.

'Thank you so much.' As I take a big swallow, I notice my hands shaking. I hate public speaking. I've always dreaded it. It's a good job Jackson sprung it on me, or I'd have been a bag of nerves all day if I'd known in advance. My hand is still trembling a little as I walk back to our table to take a seat.

A few people have vacated their seats, so Margot and Stella come to join us, both of them beaming. 'So, those lovely little flowers have saved the day, eh, darlings?' Margo says as she sits down.

'Yes, I've been meaning to ask you about the café being called Clary's, that's after the flowers, I take it?' I ask.

'Yes, darling, apparently, when the café was built, the owners called it Clary's after the flowers because they are so beautiful. Obviously, we kept the name when we bought it. I had no idea they were protected, though. Excellent news for us all.'

'Has Richard had any news about selling his business yet, Jess?' asks Dicky.

'Yeah, the company who originally wanted it, is having it. His profit isn't what it was, and they know he's desperate, so they have bid far less than the original offer. It's better than nothing, and he doesn't seem too bothered, he said that the sooner it's gone, the better. It will mean that he has to do a lot of the work on the barn himself. Plus, all the work on the farmhouse too. He seems happy with it, though. I think he's excited about it all, to be honest. He's looking forward to getting his hands dirty.' She's smiling so much it's a wonder she hasn't got a face ache.

'I'll get us another drink, then you can tell us where you figure in these plans, Jess?' I take their glasses and go to the bar.

When I sit back down, Jess says, 'I don't know yet, to be honest. When he speaks about the future he says "we." But we're taking it slow and seeing what happens.'

'Since when have you ever taken anything slow?' Dicky laughs.

'Since I'm bothered enough to want it to work out. I don't want it to be just a fling. We get on really well, and I like him. A lot.' She beams and takes a big gulp of wine.

'He feels the same, I take it?' Dicky cocks her head to one side as she asks.

'I think so. He's told me that I am helping to make staying on the farm and starting a new business fresh and exciting. So...' She trails off, and for the first time since I've known her, she blushes and looks a bit coy.

'Oh Jess is in love!' I know it's childish, but she deserves a bit of ribbing.

'Shut up, Jo!' She laughs. 'And keep your voice down! You're like a bleeding ship's fog horn. I like him, that's all. He's not a bad person. He regrets how he behaved before his dad died. It was the stress of working very long hours and still not being able to save his business. He had to let his staff go months before, so the hours were crippling him. But I could see the nice man within.' She winks and grins. 'Anyway, I've gotta be off.'

After Jess exits the pub, I talk a few of my worries over with Dicky.

'I wouldn't want to piss on her fireworks, but don't you think Jess is falling for Richard a bit too hard and a bit too quick?'

'Oh, I dunno, no quicker than me and you?' She smiles and gently elbows me in the ribs.

'Who said I was falling for you?' I elbow her back playfully.

'Sorry, only joking, what is it you're worried about?'

'It's just that men can be bastards, can't they? What if he's using her to help up on the farm, then he decides to bin her off and break her heart?'

'It's not just men who can be bastards, I can assure you. She seems happy, so I guess we just need to let her be happy. Besides, I've known Jess a long time, and she's no fool. If she thinks Richard's the one, then we have to respect that.'

'I guess you're right.' I can't help but worry a little and hope that I'm worrying for nothing. It's probably just my experience with shit head, making me distrust Richard's motives. Well, I'm certainly not gonna voice any of this to Jess, and risk her wrath. So, it's a case of, what will be, will be. He would have to go a long way to find someone better. She's pretty, bubbly, funny, and fun. What more could he want?

CHAPTER 18

BOOT SCOOTIN' BOOGIE – BRAND NEW MAN

Just as Jackson promised, we are having a country and western night. Jackson is getting quite excited, as it is his favourite kind of music. I can hear the rumble and clatter of a tractor approaching when Jackson virtually runs outside. 'Keiron! Come and give me a hand, lad.' They lug big bales of hay through the bar and into the beer garden for people to sit on.

'How the hell am I going to meet the man of my dreams, Jackson, I'm covered in bloody straw! These jeans are Hugo sodding Boss!'

'Stop being such an old woman, it'll dust off.' Jackson belly laughs, and Keiron tuts, pulling a piece of straw from his hair.

Tammy looks a bit pissed off. 'Jackson! This floor has just been cleaned, for goodness' sake!' She has a sleeping Willow on her back in a sling. 'He can sweep this up, and don't you do it either, Jo.'

'I wasn't going to,' I say, laughing. I don't think Tammy realises that, no matter how much they sweep, it'll just get walked back into the place throughout the evening. I'm not going to tell her and upset her even more. The band will be setting up soon, so I need Jackson to stop messing about with hay bales and come back into the bar, so I can go home and get ready. Eventually he comes back, dusting hay from his jumper, grinning like the cat that got the cream.

'Didn't you mention you were having hay delivered to Tammy? She said you've got to sweep the floor before any customers come in, by the way.' I have to smile because he looks so chuffed with himself.

'Aye, I did tell her, pet, but I don't think she was listening.' He winks at me, making me think he hasn't told her at all, probably because she'd have said no. 'She'll be fine when she's line dancing tonight. She's not had a proper night out in nearly a year. It'll be good for her to let her hair down, she likes to party, my old lady. Can you help put this bunting around the stage and the fences, flower?' He hands me a massive bag of multi-coloured bunting and drawing pins.

I leave Jackson sweeping up the bar and go into the garden with the bunting. There's enough to fill Kew Gardens, for goodness' sake. He doesn't do anything by halves, that's for sure. Putting the bag down, I stand, surveying the garden, and with a sigh, I crack on. Just as he asked, I put the bunting around the stage. I've never liked step ladders, or ladders of any description, so this is done on shaky legs and holding the bunting in my teeth. I then put bunting all over the fences and around each table, which me and Keiron move to the outer edges, so the bales of hay can go in a circle in the middle of the garden. I stand back to admire my work. I must admit, it looks great. I wish I had some cowboy boots. When I look at my watch, I realise it's took me much longer than I thought. Shit, I need to go and get ready!

I try on several different combinations of my take on a country and western theme. I settle for some denim shorts, a checked shirt and an old cowboy hat I've borrowed from Jackson. Yee haw!

Well, the night started well. The garden is full of people with more checked shirts than you can shake a stick at. To Jess' delight, Richard is here, looking extremely handsome in bum-hugging jeans, the oblig-atory checked shirt, and a cowboy hat. People have clearly started to warm to him because whenever I pass by, he is being asked lots of questions about what he is doing with the farm. As he talks, he has one hand on Jess' back, and she is smiling up at him.

Dicky looks very sexy in jeans, cowboy boots, a white, slightly see-through t-shirt, and cowboy hat. She seems to suit anything, but then again, she would look good in a bin bag. It amazes me how many people have managed to look the part. Have they all gone out and bought new gear, or did they all just have it hanging around in the wardrobe? I suspect it's the latter because some of them look like their outfits were around when John Wayne got off his horse to drink some milk.

The band is playing 'Cotton Eye Joe', and Jess goes to the front to lead the line dancing. It looks simple enough. 'Come on!' I pull Dicky up to join in. This is great fun and so funny, as it's not as simple as some people make it look! When they are going left, I go right. 'Shit, sorry.' Luckily, the man whose toe I just trod on, laughs.

Halfway through the song, the entire garden goes black: lights, music, the whole lot. Jackson raises his hands. 'Okay, folks, hang about, I'll go and make a call and find out what's going on.' He takes his phone from his back pocket and goes inside. When he returns, he looks really fed up. 'Sorry, everyone, but it looks like we're going to have to postpone and call it a night. There's a power cut that can't be fixed. Apparently, one of the cables is down, so they will have to wait until tomorrow to work on it. I'm sorry, but could you all just leave the premises slowly, as we don't want any accidents in the dark.' He starts to usher people out.

'Hold on! Just wait a sec,' Richard calls, weaving through the bales of hay towards Jackson. I can see him talking to Jackson, and Jackson's Stetson nodding away. He then slaps Richard on the back in a friendly gesture.

'Okay, if you're prepared to wait half an hour, we might have the answer in the shape of Richard 'ere.' The mood seems to perk up, as we wait to see what the answer actually is.

'We need some muscle to help us go up to the farm and bring a generator back down.' Lots of men stand up to go and help. 'We still won't have the beer pumps, but we've got bottles and spirits, so we should be alright. Don't light any candles though 'cause these bales of hay will go up like nobody's business. We'll be as quick as we can.' A line of men follow him out of the gate.

The chatter and laughter starts up again, and no one seems too bothered. I stumble through people to go inside the bar to check if Tammy is okay. Tammy is instructing the bar staff to light lots of tea candles around the room, but not to let anyone take any outside, and I help her make a massive vat of cocktail to be sold by the ladleful.

Over the loud chatter in the garden, we hear the sound of a tractor and trailer rattling down the lane. There's much shouting of instructions, as people have to move bales of hay out of the way to get the generator to the back of the stage. Twenty minutes or so, later, there's a loud hum of the generator starting up, and a big cheer goes up as the lights around the garden come back on. The band members take their places on the stage, and everyone laughs as they sing a few lines of, 'Light up, light up.' They stop and thank Richard for coming to the rescue.

This is so much fun. I think country music might be my new favourite! Who would've guessed it? As 'Boot Scootin' Boogie' starts up, I grab me and Dicky another one of Tammy's cocktails, even though a little voice in my head is telling me that I've had enough. Actually, the little voice is getting quite slurred, so I can't hear it properly.

I wake up in bed with the worst headache of my life! My stomach is churning, and I think I'm gonna be sick! I feel movement on the other side of my bed, and I open my eyes with a start. Dicky is lying next to me. Phew, thank God for that. I look under the covers, and I still have my bra, pants, and socks on.

'Good morning, starshine, how are you feeling?' she asks with a smirk on her face.

'Bloody terrible. I can't remember getting home, or

anything much, to be honest,' I say, holding my head in my hands.

'I helped you home, which is just as well because I don't think you'd have made it on your own. Good job there aren't many houses near here, as you were singing at the top of your lungs.' She laughs.

'Stop! Please don't tell me anything else!' I groan and close my eyes in embarrassment. I get up to go to the loo, and I look out the window as I pass. 'Dicky, who has put a wheelbarrow in my front garden?' I think I know the answer, even before she speaks.

'Erm me.' She laughs even harder. 'That was your transport home last night.'

I stop dead in my tracks. 'Please tell me you're kidding!' I have a vague memory now she's said it. 'I'm never drinking again!' I hear her laugh, and say, 'Yeah, yeah!' as I leave the room.

'Hey, don't feel obliged, but I'm fetching Meadow today to bring her to the beach. If you're not busy, you could perhaps come with us?'

'That would be nice, thanks for asking. I'd love to meet her.' I feel excited that she thinks enough of me to ask me to meet her little girl.

I'm nervous about meeting her. What if she doesn't like me? I don't have much experience with little children. Well, I need to make sure that she does like me. When Dicky has gone to fetch her, I prepare a picnic that a three year old will think is pure heaven. Light on the sandwiches and heavy on the sausage rolls, cake, biscuits, and pop front. I nearly add a bottle of wine, then I remember that I said I'm never drinking again.

Also, I'm not sure if it's irresponsible to drink when in charge of a toddler. Yes, better leave it out.

Later, when I'm alone in my cottage, I think back on the day and realise what a lovely time I've had. Eating ice cream, building sandcastles with moats and all, paddling in the sea, and Dicky taught Meadow to stand up on a surfboard, which amazed me! I got the most beautiful photo of Meadow and Dolly on the surfboard, gently riding a wave.

Dicky gave me a short surfing lesson, as promised. After many failed attempts, with me plopping into the surf like a baby seal (much to Meadow's delight), I did stand up on the board and ride a wave as Meadow sat on the beach shouting instructions. So cute. I definitely want to do it again. If only I had longer, I could've mastered it, I'm sure of it.

Meadow is such a bright little thing and asked if I'm Mummy's girlfriend. I laughed and said, 'Well, I am a girl, and I am her friend, so I guess so.' She nodded and said, 'Okay.' I looked at Dicky, who smiled with approval.

I've come home to shower all the sea salt and sand off me, and I sit on the bed, feeling suddenly tired. Aren't three year olds exhausting? I've had such a lovely day, and it just felt so right being with them both.

I check my emails, only to discover yet another rejection from an employer. For fuck's sake, I might not be here much longer. I have literally tried everywhere for a job! I have tried within one hour's drive, then extended that to one and a half hours. That would make it a three hour commute every day, any further, and I would be away from the bay all week, anyway. I haven't spoken to Dicky about it properly. She knows that I'm looking for another job, but I haven't told her that I can't afford the cottage if it doesn't happen, really soon.

Jackson is putting some feelers out but hasn't come up with anything yet. He's given me a few more shifts, bless him, but it still isn't really enough. Plus, my room at the pub has now been rented out for several months, so that's not even an option. I've spoken to our Vicky about it all, and she said I can stay with them. Good of her, I know, but the thought of it fills me with dread. We have only just started to form a sisterly relationship, and I can't help but worry that me moving in would kill that dead. 'Come on, Mum, help me out here, please,' I whisper.

I shower, and make myself look presentable, shaking off my low mood before heading over to Dicky's. We sing nursery rhymes while making spaghetti. I can't help but compare this evening to the last time I was here. Tonight is completely different, obviously, but I love it all the same, and I want this to be part of my life. Sadly, that's not looking very promising.

Meadow is in bed, having listened and joined in with every little book she owns. 'She's such a lovely little girl, isn't she?'

'She is, but you wait until you see her have a meltdown.'

I decide to wait until tomorrow to tell Dicky that my time in the bay may be limited, unless a miracle happens.

'I'm gonna head back. Thank you for a lovely day, I've really had a great time.'

'Thank you for joining us and for the picnic. Meadow loved it, and so did I.' She walks to the door with me and kisses me goodnight. 'Come back and have breakfast with us in the morning, if you'd like?'

'Yes okay, I'd like that. I don't like Coco Pops, though.'

She laughs. 'See you in the morning.'

Heading back to Dicky's flat in the morning, it is with a heavy heart. Ever since I realised that I may have to go, everything looks even more beautiful, and that includes Dicky herself, if that were possible.

Meadow is playing with some dolls, so now seems good a time as any, and I just blurt it out. 'Dicky, the thing is —' She looks at me with her beautiful smiley eyes. '—the thing is, it's not looking very likely that I can stay in the bay.'

'What? Are you kidding?' Her smile has gone, and she comes over to sit next to me, taking my hand.

'I can't find a job that pays enough for me to keep the cottage, or to keep myself, to be honest. Our Vicky and James have said I can stay with them for a little while. James, Vicky's husband, is going to set me up with a part-time office job at his place.' She's shaking her head. Her disappointment comes off her in waves.

'No, look, I need some help at the café, with that and the pub, you'll be okay.'

I shake my head. 'You don't, Dicky. You don't need any help at the café. It would be charity, and I can't do that. Thank you, though. It means a lot to me.'

'So, that's it then. Sounds like you've made up your mind. How long have we got?' she asks, her eyes full of tears.

'I guess so, yes. I will need to give Stella a few weeks' notice on the cottage. If there was any way to stay, I would stay, you know.' She goes to speak, but I cut her off. 'I can't work for you when you don't even need the help. It's bad enough that Jackson has given me more shifts, which I suspect he didn't really need covering.' She holds me in her arms, and I've never felt so at home, or so unhappy.

This feels like the worst day ever since I came to the bay just a few short months ago. It feels like only a few weeks but also like forever at the same time.

CHAPTER 19
KEEP YOUR HEAD UP – ANDY GRAMMER

As I'm walking to work, I see a bit of a commotion outside the pub. The delivery man is dropping off supplies, and he has Jake O'Brien by the scruff of his neck, shaking the shit out of him. The man is twice his size, but Jake is lashing out and swearing. I quicken my step, and as I approach them, Jackson comes out of the pub, clearly having heard the ruckus.

'What's going on 'ere, Bill?' Jackson says to the delivery man.

'I just caught this yob nicking nuts.'

'Okay, let me have him. Come inside, Jake, and Jo, go and put the kettle on, pet.' I do as I'm asked, and Jackson leads a very red-faced and shaken Jake into the pub.

I take the tea outside where Jackson and Jake are sitting at a table in the back garden, and Jackson speaks in a calm voice to Jake, who has his head in his hands. I put their teas on the table and leave them to it.

Once Jake has gone, sans the peanuts, we have one of

our little 'staff meetings'. I use the term 'staff meeting' in the loosest of terms because it's actually just me, Jess, Tammy, and Jackson sitting having a chat and a cuppa.

'Well, he admitted to the theft. All of it. The milk from the doorsteps, stuff from the shop, the lot.' Jackson is stirring his tea and has a sad expression on his face.

'The thieving little bastard' This is Jess obviously.

'Aye, well, hold on, let me tell you what he told me. You might not be so mad about it then.'

'Ah, got a sob story, has he? We've all got one of them, doesn't mean we go nicking off our own though, does it? Why couldn't he nick from town?' Jess takes a biscuit from the plate and bites it.

'Have you called the police, love?' asks Tammy while rocking Willow back and forth in her pram.

'No, I haven't, and I won't be either, and what I tell you stays between us an' all. Don't be repeating it because if nosey old Mrs Pete gets wind of it, it'll be all around the bay before lunch time.' We all nod, and he continues.

'Young Jake has been taking food to feed his younger brother and sister. His old Mum is alcohol-dependant, so what little money they have coming in, she spends on cheap booze. Anyway, he's been bunking off school to look after her and stealing to put food on the table. I've had a good talk with the lad, and I told him that I was in a similar place to him when I was his age, and that he needs to choose his path. He doesn't want to end up in prison, so anyway, I hope you'll agree with me because I've taken him on.'

'In what capacity, love?' Tammy looks a bit worried.

'I'm not sure exactly, it won't be much, but he can

wash pots, help Kieron and Steph in the kitchen, do a bit of tidying in the garden, cut the grass for us, and hopefully, for some of the neighbours, that sort of thing. He's up for it, and if he earns a bit of money, he won't have to nick stuff, will he? I want you all to give him the kind of respect you would give to any new member of our staff.' He looks directly at Jess when he says this.

Tammy gets up to give him a big hug. 'You really are a big softy, and that's why I love you.' Jess puts her arms around him and Tammy, saying, 'Me too.'

I get up and join the group hug. 'Me three!' I say, and I can feel a lump in my throat.

'A bit of a tea leaf was you then, Jackson?' Jess asks, as she pulls away.

'Nay, lass, but I was a bit free with my fists, and could easily have ended up in a whole heap of trouble. Luckily, someone gave me a leg up, and that's exactly what we're going to do for Jake. Whether or not he takes it is entirely up to him.' Tammy gives a little cough to gain Jackson's attention. 'Oh, aye, and my good lady here put me on the straight and narrow an all.'

'Oh, yes, that reminds me. Tell Jo how you two got together. It's so romantic.' Jess is looking from Jackson to Tammy.

'Nothing much to tell, and it's not very romantic. Tammy was having a bit of trouble with a fella, so I pushed him onto his backside.' Jackson chuckles and shrugs his shoulders.

'There was a bit more to it than that.' Tammy laughs. 'What he actually did was come over and said, "Excuse me, young lady, would you like some assistance?" The man I was with did not take too kindly to this big stranger stepping between us, and he made the mistake of taking a swing at Jackson. Jackson could've knocked him clean out, but he chose not to. I knew right then that this was the man I was going to marry.'

Keiron, who has come through from the kitchen, and is putting salt and pepper pots on the tables says, 'Be still, my beating heart.' Holding his hand on his chest.

'Ah, see, how romantic is that?' Jess rests her chin on her hand, looking all dreamy.

All three of us laugh, and she looks from one to the other and says, 'What's funny?'

'Right, anyway, I better get down that cellar for a stock check.' Jackson gets up, taking his empty mug with him.

'Yes, I'm taking this little lady to baby massage. See you all later.' Tammy waves and pushes Willow through the front door.

'So, how's the barn conversion coming on?' I'm kinda putting off telling her that I'm leaving.

'It's all happening so quick!' The excitement in her voice is obvious. 'Richard works so hard and helps out the builders, he's really impressive actually, he knows loads of stuff, and he's dead strong.' I laugh at her, and she gives me the middle finger. 'Anyway, we've had some bookings for a wedding, well, two weddings actually, and a conference, even before it's finished!'

'Erm, "we've" had some bookings?' I raise my eyebrows.

'Erm, yes, I've got something to tell you. The first wedding is mine.' She fiddles with her cup. When she looks up, the joy in her eyes makes mine fill with tears (again).

'Oh my God, oh my God! He's asked you to marry him? When? How did he ask you? You've obviously said yes?' I jump up, and so does she. We hug, squealing and laughing, but we have tears rolling down our faces, too.

'What's all this about?' Jackson has just come into the bar from the cellar.

'Richard has asked me to marry him, and I've said yes!' Jess does a little jog on the spot, and Jackson comes to hug her. 'I'm happy for you, lass, I really am. Richard, seems like a good bloke.'

'You're not looking very surprised, Jackson. You already knew, didn't you?' Jess says with a surprised look on her face. 'You did! How did you know?'

"Well, Richard is a bit old-fashioned, as it 'appens, and he asked what my thoughts were, about asking you, in the absence of a father, you see.'

'Oh my God, how lovely!' I feel so emotional. I look at Jess, who is looking at Jackson with such pride. 'You said you like the idea, I take it? I guess that means you'll be wanting to give me away then?'

'Aye, it does, to the first silly beggar that has the gumption to take you on,' he says, and he kisses Jess on the top of her head before walking away. Just like my dad used to do to me. And this is my undoing. Tears, snot, the lot.

'Hey, what's up with you?' Jess asks, looking alarmed.

'Nothing, nothing at all. I'm just happy for you,' I say, wiping my nose on my sleeve.

'Well, good because you're my bridesmaid, or is it matron of honour at your age?' She winks, and I manage to laugh through my tears. God, I love these people so much. What's it been? Just months not years, and yet, I'm being asked to be a bridesmaid? I've found love and genuine friendship that will kill me to leave behind. I can't tell her right now. I don't want to pop her happy little bubble.

'When is the big day? When will the barn be finished?'

'Five weeks, on my birthday, October 25th. I need a dress, which I need help to choose, so obviously, you need to come shopping with me.' Her excitement is rubbing off on me.

'Absolutely! And why so quick?' I look at her stomach with raised eyebrows.

'No! Don't be daft, nothing like that. We just decided to be the first to christen the barn when it's finished. Richard said, "Why wait?" When you know, you know, and I know Jo.' She squeaks, and we hug again.

Whenever we get a lull in customers, the talk is all about the imminent wedding. I was a bag of nerves before mine and wanted everything just perfect. Jess, on the other hand, is the complete opposite. She isn't tress or bridezillar-ish at all. She's so laid back, doesn't want any fuss, only a small and quiet affair. Pah, as if! Not on her nelly. The Jess I know and love will lavish the attention and is a the-more-the-merrier kind of girl.

She chatters about their plans for the farm, and Richard has given her free rein to make plans for a second barn, although she is undecided as to what it could be. I suggested a petting zoo, but she turns her nose up, claiming that animals smell, and she's not keen on having a load of kids running around. She gets out her notepad, and there are pages of ideas and scribbles. She thought of a café, but then rejected the idea, as she doesn't want to step on Dicky's toes. I have no doubt she will come up with a genius idea before very long.

I need to tell her sooner rather than later that I'm leaving the bay. I'll be going a day or so after her wedding, so it's about time she knew. I would hate for her to hear it from someone else.

When I tell Stella, she is sadder than I thought she would be. 'Oh, lovey, that's so sad!' she exclaims. 'I thought you were here to stay. You've become part of our lovely bay.' She pats my hand and rubs my arm when I start to cry. 'You've done such a lovely job on the garden too. I, for one, will be very sad to see you go and I'll miss you, and even more so by a few others, I suspect.'

'I'm so sorry, Stella, I hoped to put down some roots here too, but I'm afraid it isn't to be. I'm sure you'll get new tenants, it's such a beautiful cottage.' I wipe my eyes and try to pull myself together.

'No, I think I'll sell the cottage if you're going. No point in keeping it. I might take Margot on an around the world cruise, pick up a few rich gents.' She laughs, and I laugh with her, relieved that she has tried to lighten the mood.

I have asked Jess to come round tonight for a glass or two of wine. I'm almost as nervous telling Jess as I was Dicky.

She's so bubbly as she comes through my front door. She looks lovely actually, happiness does that to a person, doesn't it? She's lost a bit of weight and her tight t-shirt shows off her big boobs and her denim cut off shorts show off her tan.

Just as I did with Dicky, I blurt it out. 'I'm leaving the bay, Jess,' I say, bursting into tears.

'Has that bastard husband of yours been back again?' She looks fuming.

'No, it's got nothing to do with him. Anyway, he'll have been served with the divorce papers by now.'

'What then? Why? You're my best friend, I don't want you to go!' She throws her hands in the air childishly, and I almost smile, but I haven't got a smile in me right now. 'Everyone leaves me. It's happened all my life! I won't let you go, Jo, I just won't. I've never had a proper friend until you came. You're like the sister I never had!' she wails.

'You'll be fine, Jess, you'll have a super new life, and Richard clearly loves you very much. I'll be back for holidays, you'll get sick of seeing me.' I pull off two pieces of kitchen roll and hand one to Jess, and we both blow our noses. 'I can't find full-time work, or part time, come to that, you know how hard I've tried. The Stern is great, and I love it, but the hours just aren't enough now my savings are all gone.'

'Oh God, this is horrible news.'

'I know, no one can be more disappointed than me. I can assure you, I'm heartbroken. I really am.'

We finish the bottle, and Jess makes some suggestions, but none are feasible. Once she has gone, I sit and have another cry. Not just a sniffle, oh no, a full-on tears and snot cry. I feel so retched. I pick up the little ballerina. 'Oh, Mum, I've failed again,' I whisper as I carefully put her back down.

~

The next day, 'Hummingbird' Tom, comes into the Stern looking as pleased as punch. 'Morning Tom, you look happy. Have you seen your hummingbird again?'

Yes, I have, and I can prove it.' He grins and quickly takes his phone from his jacket pocket. I hope it's not more pictures of his eye. He hands the phone over the bar, and I open up his pictures. I have done some research on hummingbirds, and I was correct, they aren't found in the UK. However, there is a day moth called a hummingbird hawk moth, which looks and hovers just like a hummingbird. It has been mistaken for it many times. When I find the pictures, I can see that they are all, in fact, pictures of the moth. 'See! What did I tell you? Right there, plain as day, that's a hummingbird.' I open my mouth to tell him, but I close it again. He looks so happy that I can't spoil it for him.

'Oh my goodness, Tom, you're right, a hummingbird! Well, I wouldn't have believed it had I not seen your pictures.'

'Beautiful, isn't it?' That gummy smile melts my heart.

'What's beautiful?' Jackson asks as he enters the bar.

'Tom's hummingbird, Jackson, he has pictures!' And under my breath I say, 'I'll explain later.'

I get a quizzical look from Jackson, but he just nods and says, 'Well done, Tom, that one must be lost.' He chuckles as he leaves the bar. I'll tell them all later and ask them not to tell him. What harm can it do? Every dog should have his day, so they say, and this day belongs to Tom.

CHAPTER 20
WHITE DRESS – PARACHUTE

Now, I don't know if you've ever been wedding dress shopping with anyone, but if you have, I bet it was nothing like wedding dress shopping with Jess! I had to persuade her to try on white or ivory and steer her away from anything purple or red. At least ten dresses later and three different shops, she was drunk as a skunk on all the free champaign! In the third shop, I'm sitting watching the cubicle curtain with baited breath. I guess she has found one that she likes, as I can hear her singing, 'I feel pretty' while the assistant asks her, 'Please stand still a moment.'

'Ta-dah!' She flings the curtain to the side, almost smacking the shop assistant in the face. 'Oops, watch yourself!' She giggles as the girl ducks out of the way.

She's swaying slightly, but she looks stunning. Jess has been doing physical work up at the farm, helping Richard, and it shows in her hour-glass figure.

She has chosen an off-the-shoulder, figure-hugging

dress, which fish tails at the bottom, and it's white, would you believe?

'What do you think?' She twirls and turns from side to side.

'I love it Jess, you look beautiful.' I tear up a bit. 'You'll need shoes.' The far side of the shop has a small rack of ivory and white satin shoes. As I'm walking towards them, she says, 'If you think I'm wearing those granny efforts, you can think again!' She shakes her head as she lifts her dress to show me her dirty pink converse.

'Absolutely not!' I say, horrified, and she laughs.

'Of course I won't be wearing these, but I won't be wearing them either!' She points at the rack of shoes. I smile at the shop assistant, who gives me a half-hearted smile back. I think she'll be glad to see the back of us, even taking into account the fact that Jess is spending a small fortune in here.

Once Jess is back in her own clothes, which involved a lot of giggling and bashing into the cubicle walls, she insists I look at bridesmaid dresses. This is the part I've been dreading. I don't really like attention, so I am glad all eyes will be on Jess on the day.

'Okay, my friend, the colour theme is white and burnt orange. So, find the style you like, and we'll have it made in burnt orange, capiche?'

Thank God I've got a tan. I am the only grown-up bridesmaid, which is a little worrying, as I was kind of hoping to blend in a bit. She had asked Dicky too, but her offer was declined, so she made her a witness instead. Willow is too young, but Meadow is a flower girl, so at least I can walk down the aisle with her.

I look at dresses that would hide most of my body,

holding one up that will cover me from neck to floor. 'Put that back! You have the most amazing pair of knockers, Jo, you need to make sure Dicky can't take her eyes off them—I mean—take her eyes off you!' she says quite loudly.

I ignore her and look at the dresses. She thrusts a halter neck dress into my arms.

'Here, try this.'

'Blimey, it's a bit low cut!' Shit a brick. Oh well, her wish is my command, for her wedding, at any rate.

Once I've got in on, I turn around to look in the mirror, I'm surprised to see it suits me quite nicely, I really like it, and it does, in fact, make my 'knockers' look amazing.

'Hello girls!' Jess exclaims, jiggling my boobs with her hands. 'You look fantastic.'

She immediately puts in an order to have it made, informing the woman that they need to make it snappy while swigging back my glass of champaign.

Jess chooses a gorgeous little white dress for Meadow, that I just know, she will look at cute as a button in.

'Right, that's the wedding shopping done. Let's get rat arsed!' she announces, kissing the shop assistant on the cheek and dragging me out the door.

'There's a lot more to a wedding than just the dresses, Jess,' I say, feeling quite worried.

'It's all in hand, Joanna, my friend, all in hand.'

I mention to Jess that I have driven here, so I can't drink, but she insists I leave my car and get Jackson to bring me to fetch it tomorrow.

Once I have left the bay, it might be a very long time

until I get to do anything like this with Jess again, so I agree to leave my car in the carpark.

There's a strip of bars in Hillside Quay, and Jess wants to hit them all. I can't let myself get too drunk, as I need to keep my eye on her.

I would've thought the bars would be empty, as it's so early, but they aren't. It's quite lively with what I guess are a few stag and hen parties milling about. As we're walking into a bar, Fred Flintstone and Barney Rubble run past us, handcuffed together, shouting, 'Yabba dabba doo.'

Oh, great, the bar has a pole, which Jess spots as soon as we walk in. I'm at the bar when I hear a cheer go up, so I turn around to see Jess has climbed onto the podium and is doing what she clearly thinks is a sexy dance around the pole. Oh God. I take the drinks to a table and out of the corner of my eye, I see her trying to swing her legs above her head, like they do in the movies. However, they know what they are doing, whereas Jess, unfortunately, does not. She slides quickly down the pole and onto her head with a thump, to some loud clapping and cheering from a group of well-oiled men.

After several cocktails, most of which were bloody horrible, I decide it's time to get this bride-to-be home. I struggle to get her out of the bar. 'Come and have a go on the pole, Jo, the boys love it!'

'I don't think so, I'd break my neck, like you almost did when you slid upside down onto your head!'

'That was all part of the act, Joanna, my friend, all part of the act.'

I finally get her to a taxi rank, only to be told by

several taxi drivers that they won't take her. Taking one look at her, they shake their heads. Can't blame them, I suppose, they must get tired of cleaning sick off the back seats of their cab.

Moving along the line of taxis, all I can say is, thank God for old Derick! He even helped me to get her into the back of his cab.

He drops us at my cottage, and I give him a large tip for his help.

'Thank you, darlin'.' Then, as he helps me get Jess out the back of the cab, he says, 'Good luck with the wedding, lovely. He's a lucky man.' He chuckles as he gets back in the car.

I sit her on the settee and try to get her to drink some water, but she gets up, wobbles to the kitchen, and tips it down the sink. 'I'm not bothering with a hen do, Jo, so this is my hen do, and you're trying to get me to drink bloody water?'

I tut and shrug, then go to pour us a glass of wine. When I return, she is crying. 'Oh Jesus, I didn't think you were one of those drunks that cry when you've had a few too many.' I try to make light of it, and I quickly go to tip away the wine and get us both a big glass of water.

'Well, I fucking am since my best friend is leaving me, by the way,' she wails. I put my arm around her, making shushing noises and listen while she tells me about her life.

'My mother, my own mother, left me at some hospital doors at one day old.' She hiccoughs and wipes her nose on her jacket.

I feel terrible for her. 'Oh, Jess, I'm so sorry.' I pull her in, and she rests her head on my shoulder.

I make promises about returning to see her regularly, that I hope I can keep. I think we both know that it won't happen often. Life gets in the way, and I couldn't bear to see Dicky with someone else.

She raises her head. 'How did your parents die, Jo?'

I let out a sigh. 'I had just finished uni and had started my dream job. As you know, I love plants and everything to do with them, and that was basically my job, learning about them, growing them, experimenting with them. Anyway, I was at work, and I got a call from my older sister, Vicky, to say a lorry had overturned in high winds, and my dad had driven straight into the back of it, killing them both instantly. He always drove fast. That was the only thing I ever heard them argue about.' I wipe tears from my eyes with my sleeve.

'God, that's terrible. You must have been devastated, poor you. Is that why you drive like an old lady?' She smiles, and I can't help but laugh a little.

'Probably. I've never thought about it. I didn't know I drove like an old lady until you pointed it out, but you could be right.' I give a weak laugh. Only Jess could joke during a conversation like this.

She surprises me by saying, 'I like plants, you know?' She puts her arm on my shoulders and continues, 'I had one foster mother that I liked a lot. Her name was Jenny. She had a garden a lot like yours. She was gardening mad, out there in all weathers, she was. She gave me a patch in a raised bed to grow veg. I refused to begin with. I was a right stroppy cow, but she didn't let up. Anyway, I learned loads from her and grew carrots and cabbage, some beans up the fence, all sorts really. I loved eating the stuff I had grown. She told me that I had green fingers.' She pulls a face and wiggles her fingers. 'I remember one Mother's Day, I bought her a gnome. He was bending over doing a moony. She loved that gnome. That was the only Mother's Day gift I ever bought.' She gives me a watery smile.

'That explains my house warming gift!' I chuckle. 'Did you stay with Jenny, then?'

'I did for quite a long time, yes. She was a lovely woman.' She sniffs.

'Was? Don't you see her anymore?'

'I would, but she died of cancer. At her funeral, the church was full of grow-up kids that she had fostered over the years. It's not fucking fair, is it?'

'No, Jess, it's not fair.'

My heart feels so heavy, and I really didn't want to think about all this today.

I fetch Jess a pillow and spare quilt, and she is asleep before I turn out the light.

CHAPTER 21
WHEREVER YOU WILL GO –
THE CALLING

I'm making Dicky a meal tonight. It's like a date, but not a date, I guess. An actual date would have the hope and promise of things to come, but now I'm leaving, the hope and promise have gone. Still, I'm looking forward to it, in a bittersweet kind of way.

When she arrives and sees all the full packing boxes in the hallway, and she gives me a sad smile. I'm determined not to let what might be our last night alone together be sad and maudlin. Dolly bounds in, wagging her little tail vigorously, so I pick her up and bury my face in her soft fur. Nobody greets you with the enthusiasm of a dog, do they? It might be weird if they did.

I've prepared slow-roasted tomato, garlic, and prawn spaghetti. When I read the recipe, it said capsicum was one of the ingredients. What in God's name is a capsicum? One thing is for sure, Meadow Cliff Bay's general store wouldn't stock it. Google informed me, it's a chilli pepper. Why didn't it just say bloody chilli pepper?

I make her laugh with the drama of the wedding dress shopping trip, filling her in on all the funny bits.

'Speaking of the wedding, I had a little rehearsal with Meadow for her duties as a flower girl.' She laughs, so I ask, 'How did that go?'

'Well, first of all, she tasted a petal. Obviously, she didn't like it, so she spat it out.' She's doing the actions, which makes me laugh.

'Then she threw them into the air like confetti, dancing around, loving life, then got bored, and just tipped the whole lot on the floor. It took me a while to get her to sprinkle them on the floor, a few at a time, as she walked. I used some chocolate as a bribe.' She shakes her head. 'Makes me a bit nervous about what she'll do on the day.'

'Don't worry too much about it, Jess will find it funny, whatever she does.'

'I hope so. Richard and Jess came into the café for lunch during the week. They were covered in paint and looked so happy together.' She sighs. 'I'm so happy for Jess, and she deserves to be happy too, but I couldn't help feeling—' she falters. 'I dunno, a bit jealous, I guess.'

'I know what you mean. I am so happy for her too, and Richard, of course. A few people got him wrong, me included. But all the excitement of the wedding is just making it harder to leave. Anyway, I'll dish up.' I stand to go through to the kitchen, and Dicky follows me. 'I'll help you,' she offers.

'Absolutely not. I'll be waiting on you tonight.'

'Sounds promising.' She smiles. God, I love her sexy smile.

Dicky pours more wine while I put, what has turned out to be, quite an impressive-looking dish on to the plates.

'This is amazing! I've never had fish with spaghetti, but it's lovely.'

'Why thank you, glad you like it.'

'You're not just a pretty face, are you?'

'And thank you some more.' I'm less embarrassed by compliments these days. I just take them, so much happier in my own skin.

After dinner, Dicky picks up my guitar. 'Come on, give me a song. I'm not taking no for an answer this time.' She hands it to me.

Putting my new found confidence to the test, I take it from her. 'What would you like me to play?'

'Anything at all. You choose.'

Doing a quick tune up and clearing my throat, I settle on 'Wherever You Will Go' by The Calling. She sings along, and I know I'll remember this moment, right here, right now, for the rest of my life.

'God, you're really good!' She sounds a little surprised.

'Thanks, I had a really good teacher.'

Taking my guitar from me, Dicky takes hold of my hand and leads me up the stairs. Dolly curls up on a blanket at the bottom of the bed and is snoring softly in seconds.

'I can't do this,' I say with tears in my eyes.

'Can't do what?' Dicky takes my hand and kisses me tenderly.

I pull away a little. 'This.' I point to the bed. 'It's hard enough to leave you as it is. If we make love again, walking away will be impossible, and anyway, I'm too sad.'

'Okay, then we won't. We can just lie together?' she asks, knowing that I won't, can't, say no.

We lie facing each other, and I can see her face clearly. The curtains aren't closed properly, so the moon is lighting the bedroom a little. I can see sorrow etched across her face. She wraps her arm around me, and her body presses against mine. Her skin is smooth, and her distinctive smell is intoxicating.

'I'll wait for you to come back. If you promise me you will come back,' she whispers.

'I would love, with all my heart, to say yes, I'll be back, but we both know that's a long shot, don't we? No work, no money, no can do as my dad used to say.' I sniff, and she wipes a tear from my cheek.

We are falling asleep, our limbs entwined. Dicky's eyes are closed, and her breathing tells me she has dropped off, so I say, 'I love you.' She takes a deep breath and whispers, 'I love you too.'

The next morning, we walk Dolly on the beach with heavy hearts. We make promises to each other that we know will be hard to keep, but it makes us feel better to say them, anyway.

Since the night we said I love you, I haven't seen much of Dicky. I think we are both trying to protect our hearts by keeping a bit of a distance. It's the morning of the wedding, and I am up early. I've been crying so much that my eyes look puffy, and my face is blotchy, so I'm giving myself a facial. I asked Jess if she wanted to stay with me the night before, as it's bad luck to see the groom before the ceremony, but Jess said, 'That's bollocks', and she refused to follow tradition. So, I'm going up to the farm to help her into her dress and to get ready myself with her.

Jess comes through my front door as I am sitting on the settee in a green face mask, which promises to revive and refresh the skin.

'Fucking hell!' she says, holding her chest when she sees me. 'You might need to do something with your face.'

'Oh har har, very funny,' I say this without moving my lips, so I don't crack the face pack. 'One minute,' I say, running upstairs to wash off the mask. Looking in the bathroom mirror, there is little improvement to my tired-looking eyes, but my skin is less blotchy, so that's a bonus.

'What are you doing here?' I ask her as I walk back into the lounge. 'It's your wedding day, aren't you supposed to be having your hair styled in an elaborate updo or something?'

'Yes, later. I've got bags of time for all that. I've come to ask you to look at something for me.' She produces a piece of paper from her jeans pocket. 'It's an ad, which I would like you to check over, you know for spelling mistakes and that before it goes online, as you're the only person I know with a university degree.' She puts it on the coffee table and goes to put the kettle on.

It reads:

Wanted: Full-Time Manager

An experienced person is wanted to help set up and manage a new garden centre. Good rate of pay.

Must have previous experience and knowledge in growing, buying, and selling plants and gardening products. The successful person must live near to Hill-Top Farm and be a very good friend of the owner. She must also be in love with the local café owner.

To apply, go into the kitchen.

I read through it three times. My heart is pounding in my chest as I walk into the kitchen. Jess is leaning on the counter.

'Is this for real, Jess?' I can hardly breathe. She nods vigorously.

'Yes, it's for real, you arse, as if I would be so cruel to joke about this! Well? What do you think? It was Richard's idea, but my idea to do the ad.' She is grinning from ear to ear.

'Well, yes, I mean absolutely, oh my God, I can't believe it, if you're sure this is what you want to do, and it's not just for my benefit?'

'Don't be daft, course it isn't just to keep you here. That's just part of it. I'm so excited about this. Does that mean you'll stay?' She takes a step towards me, and I wrap my arms around her.

'Yes, yes, yes! Thank you, I honestly don't know what to say, Jess.' I start to cry again. I seem to be doing a lot of it lately. And Jess cries too. 'Right, stop crying. We can't have you all puffy-eyed on your big day.'

'No, I know. I need to tell Richard, and you need to let Stella know, so she doesn't put the cottage on the market.'

'Well, I might ask for first refusal. Now I'll be a manager! Plus, and this is big news, Tony has agreed to buy me out of the house, so I'll have a deposit!' I jump up and down, hardly able to contain my excitement. 'Hold on, when did you decide to have a garden centre up there?'

'Literally yesterday! Richard wants me to be happy of course. I'd already told him about Jenny, my foster mother, and her getting me into gardening, he knows what work you used to do, so he suggested it. I love it, this is the icing on my wedding cake!'

Jess takes her phone from her pocket and sends a text. She then goes to the front door and retrieves a carrier bag from the doorstep.

'Ta-dah! Time to celebrate!' She produces a bottle of champagne from the bag, takes three glasses from the cupboard, pops the cork, and fills each glass.

'Why three glasses, Jess?' I ask as Dicky bursts through the door.

'Did she say yes?' She looks at Jess. 'Did you say yes?' she squeals as she runs into the kitchen.

'YES!' both Jess and I shout at the same time.

'Oh my god, oh my god.' She picks me up and twirls me around, which is no mean feat, I can assure you.

We have a three-way hug, and each of us is laughing and crying at the same time.

Jess pulls away and says, 'Right, I gotta go. This day is the best ever already! I woke up to an amazing shag with my husband to be, and my best friend is not only staying in the bay, but we are going to be working together! My whole life I have wondered what it would be like to have a sister, and now I know!' We all hug

186

again, and she leaves after knocking back the entire contents of her glass of champaign.

When we're alone, Dicky and I stand looking at each other for a second or two without moving. 'You already knew? You knew Jess was going to offer me the job?'

'Only since this morning. I dropped Meadow at my mum's, and I have been pacing around the flat waiting for her text. I could hardly hang in my skin.' She takes a deep shuddering breath and says, 'I can't begin to tell you how happy I feel.'

'I meant what I said when we were last in bed together,' I say, feeling a little out of breath.

'Which part?' She gives me a knowing but ever so sexy smile.

'You know which part.' I put my hands in my dressing gown pockets, suddenly feeling a little self-conscious.

'I want to hear you say it again.' She takes a couple of steps towards me before stopping and looking me in the eye, as if she can see into my soul.

I remove my hands from my pockets. 'I love you.' I close the gap between us, and as my lips find hers, I hear her say, 'Right back atcha.'

CHAPTER 22

AT LAST – ETTA JAMES

The entire village is either inside the church or outside in the courtyard, waiting to get a look at the bride.

It is warm for the time of year, and the weather is perfect. The grave yard is the ideal backdrop of autumnal colours with the leaves on the trees varying shades of yellow, brown, and orange. It matches the burnt orange accent colour of the wedding nicely. The photos are going to look amazing.

Me and Meadow are waiting at the church doors for Jess to arrive with Jackson.

As Jess steps out of the shiny black Daimler, there is a cheer from the awaiting crowd. A little boy, who obviously can't wait until the ceremony is over, runs up and throws a handful of confetti at Jess. She chuckles and picks a bunch of it out of her cleavage and throws it back at him, which makes everyone laugh and clap.

Jess looks stunning. Her dress hugs her shapely figure in all the right places, and the hairdresser has woven white and orange flowers through her hair, which is pinned up, apart from a few curls falling onto her bare shoulders. As she takes the arm of a very handsome, suited and booted, Jackson to walk down the aisle, I struggle not to cry happy tears as my absolute joy threatens to spill over.

'Come on, honey,' I say to Meadow. 'We have to go in, so you can sprinkle your petals for Jess to walk on.'

Meadow looks so cute in her little white dress with tutu underskirts, making it stick out and shows off her chubby little legs. I notice she has little silver converse on her feet. I turn to Jess, who smiles as she sees where I'm looking. She winks at me and lifts her dress to reveal matching silver converse. I widen my eyes and laugh. I love this girl so much.

Me and Meadow walk down the aisle ahead of Jess and Jackson. The little girl does quite a good job with the petals, that is, until she gets to her grandmother, Margot, and she says, 'These are for you, Mama!' She gives her a handful of petals.

'Thank you, darling.' Margot laughs, as does the rest of the congregation. Margot's choice of outfit, does not disappoint, as she has on a multicoloured kaftan, with a bright orange bird of paradise fascinator in her hair.

Meadow and I take our places at the front as 'At Last' by Etta James begins to play. Jess and Jackson come into view and the whole congregation turn to look at her. I immediately look at Richard, who looks so handsome in a navy-blue suit, complete with burnt orange pocket square and corsage. Everyone looks at the bride as she walks down the aisle, don't they? But I always look at the groom. That's when you see it, and today, I saw it. He took the deepest of breaths, and the love shining out of his eyes was palpable.

As they reach the front, Jackson gives Richard Jess' hand, and I can read his lips as Richard whispers, 'You're so beautiful.' Oh boy, right on cue, the big tears appear.

After the ceremony, Dicky drives me and Meadow to the farm.

'Come on, let's go and eat, drink, and be merry! You both look very pretty, by the way,' she says as we get into her car. 'Thank you, Mummy, so do you.'

'Yes, you do.' I lean over and kiss her on the cheek.

Dicky is wearing a blue trouser suit with a cream camisole top underneath, which shows off her lovely olive coloured skin.

The barn looks absolutely gorgeous. It has high beams, white walls, big round tables covered in white table cloths, each with tiny pumpkins and autumn leaves as the centre piece. The seats have white covers tied in bows at the back with burnt orange satin. The stage is set up with amplifiers and various instruments, ready for the band. Wedding venues don't come more romantic than this. Jess obviously has a flare for this sort of thing.

There isn't a traditional top table, but the front and centre table is reserved for the wedding party, which consists of Jess, Richard, Richard's best man (Harry), Jackson, Tammy, Willow, Dicky, Meadow, and me. I feel so happy and honoured to be sitting here and to have a part in Jess and Richards' special day.

The meal is delicious. I opted for brown butter sole with peas and mussels, which is cooked in a local cider. Dicky opted for the ale-glazed beef fillet with a crispy onion crust. She takes a forkful of beef and leans over. 'Try this, it's amazing.'

'Oh my god, it is delicious, here try mine.' I give her a forkful of sole. 'Yes, lovely, but I'm glad I chose this.' She points to her beef. I must say, both dishes are Gordon Ramsey worthy.

Harry's speech is hilarious and quite camp. He's tall, very slim, and gesticulates a lot when he speaks. Jess told me he was gay, and he comes into his own when he takes the mic to talk about Richard and their years growing up together.

'Good evening, lovely people. If I could just have your attention for a few minutes, that would be super. Me and the main man here have been friends since we were thirteen years old. Between me and you, I don't think he's very astute, as it took him six years to figure out that I'm gay!' Everyone laughs, including Richard. 'He tried to set me up with so many girls, and I always gave him the same answer. She isn't my type, sweetheart. I remember well, having had this very conversation with him for the hundredth time, I kid you not, when I saw the penny drop!' More laughter, and Richard shrugs his shoulders. I notice Keiron's interest is piqued, as he's laughing loudly and doesn't take his eyes off Harry.

Harry continues, 'Isn't he handsome? Such a waste that he's straight.' Richard bats his hand playfully, in a slack wrist way, and more laughter ensues.

'Anyway, I only met Jess for the first time a couple of weeks ago, and I fell in love with her immediately.' He looks at Jess, who smiles at him shaking her head.

'The very first thing she said to me was, "I'm prob- ably going to be seeing quite a lot of you, so let's get rat arsed and see what kind of drunk you are." From that very moment, we got on like a house on fire!' Over the laughter, he raises his glass and says, 'To the bride and groom, may your problems be little ones, and may your happiness know no bounds!' Everyone toasts the happy couple, and as Harry sits down, Jackson gets to his feet.

'I'll keep this short and sweet. I would just like to say, I am filled with pride at the amazing woman Jess has become. Tammy and I have watched you grow from a stroppy teenager into a funny, confident, happy woman who knows what she wants and goes out and gets it. We love you very much. And Richard? You look after her now, won't you?'

'I will indeed, Jackson, you have my word.' Richard shakes Jacksons hand as he stands. 'I would like to thank you all for coming to share our day. I've never believed people, when they say that their wedding day was the happiest day of their life. But today is absolutely the happiest day of my life.' He then turns to Jess, 'My darling Jessica, I promise to spend the rest of my life making you as happy as you have made me by agreeing to be my wife. Could everyone stand and raise your glasses to my beautiful wife, Jessica!' Everyone stands, and there is a loud chorus of, 'to my beautiful wife Jessica!' The room erupts into laughter.

Breaking with tradition, Jess takes to her feet to say a few words. She is radiating happiness and confidence.

'Richard, I love you so much, and I promise to walk by your side, hand in hand with you in everything we do. Jackson and Tammy, I will be forever grateful that you made me part of your family. You took a wayward teenager and taught me what love is, thank you. Lastly, I want to thank all of you for coming and just to say, friends old and new, I love you all. Oh, and Richard? You look well fit! Now, let's drink and dance the night away!'

Richards laughs, and everyone stands to give a raucous round of applause.

The band plays 'Turn Me On' by Nora Jones as Jess and Richard take to the floor for their first dance as man and wife. Half way through the song, other couples join in, so Dicky takes my hand, leading me onto the floor in what I can only say is the happiest dance of my life. This is made extra special by the fact that, after a few moments, we have Meadow between us, sitting on Dicky's hip with a little fat arm draped around each of our shoulders.

The party Is just getting started when I see a woman standing in the barn's doorway that I recognise. Oh my God, it's our Vicky! I virtually run over to her.

'What are you doing here? When did you get here? Do you want a drink?' My questions tumble out as I give her a big hug.

She laughs. 'I've just got here. I went to the Stern and the barmaid said you'd be here. I hope your friend won't mind me gate-crashing her wedding?'

'Don't be daft, of course she won't. I'll get you some champagne.'

'Erm, no thanks, an orange and soda please?'

'Orange and soda? No Champagne?' I squint at her.

'I'm not drinking at the moment, not for the next six months anyway, Auntie Jo.' She looks down at her belly with a huge smile on her face.

'Oh my God, you're pregnant!' I hug her again. 'Congratulations! Why didn't you tell me?'

'That's why I came, to give you my good news!'

This day just gets better and better! I can honestly say this is the best wedding ever!

I take Vicky to our table and introduce her to Dicky. While Dicky is distracted by Meadow wanting more cake, Vicky looks at me and says, 'Very nice.'

I go to get us some drinks, and Keiron and Harry are standing at the bar, talking and laughing together.

When I return to the table, Dicky's phone rings.

'I won't be a minute.' She speaks for a moment into her phone, then she goes over and says something to her mum before leaving the barn. She then comes back with a heavy-set man that can only be her dad. She introduces him to me. 'This is my dad, Vic. Dad, this is my girl-friend, Joanna.' Girlfriend, eh? Wow. 'And this is her sister Vicky.'

He is the absolute spit, albeit the male version of Dicky, with darker skin and a lovely smile. He gives me a bear hug. 'I've heard a lot about you, Joanna. Glad you're making my daughter so happy. It's about time, eh, bebi-ta?' He puts a big hand on Dicky's shoulder and kisses her cheek. He turns to Vicky. 'Nice to meet you too, Vicky.' He takes her hand and kisses it. What a charmer.

'Dad, you remember Meadow?' Meadow has come up to us to see who he is.

'Of course, I remember, how you've grown! I'm Vic, your grandad.' He takes her little hand in his and kisses it too.

Meadow says a very shy hello, wiping the back of her hand down her dress. Aren't little kids funny? Then, off she runs to join another little girl that she's been playing with for most of the evening.

As time wears on, I'm feeling a little worse for the champaign that's been flowing in my direction all night, so I sit and look around the room at these lovely people, many of whom I can now call good friends. Our Vicky is making herself at home, chatting away at the bar to Keiron and Harry. I don't think she realises that she's probably getting in the way. I'll rescue them in a bit.

Vic is now on the dance floor (fast worker), twirling Stella and Margot around, all three laughing and seemingly having a ball, obviously putting any differences to one side for tonight.

Jackson and Tammy are having a smooch, looking at each other with a love that can only make any onlooker smile.

Jess is sitting on Richard's knee, swaying to the music with a bottle of Champagne in her hand, and both are looking as happy as they should be on their wedding day.

The band plays a cover of 'Forever My Love' by Ed Sheeran and J Balvin.

Dicky takes my hand and leads me outside to dance by the light of the moon with the surf lapping down below the cliff top. As we move slowly to the music, Dicky winks at me and gives me that smile that never ceases to make my heart pound.

As the song ends, I stand, looking out over the moonlit sea. Dicky moves behind me and puts her arms around me, resting her head on my shoulder.

'I'm so happy you're staying Jo. I love you so much.'

'Me too, more than you can imagine.' I look up at the stars and think of my mum looking down on me and smiling. I know it might be a coincidence, but I'm sure one of those stars just winked at me.

The End. 😊

The Meadow Cliff Bay Play List
I Will Survive – Gloria Gaynor
What a Difference the Day Makes – Ester Phillips
House of the Rising Sun – The Animals
I kissed a Girl – Katy Perry
Take It Outside – Brantley Gilbert
Bad Moon Rising – Creedence Clearwater Revival
Stand By Me – Ben E King
In the Living Years – Mike & the Mechanics
Ride the Wild Surf – Jan & Dean
Taking Care of Business – Bachman Turner Overdrive
A Whiter Shade of Pale – Annie Lennox
Sweet Child of Mine – Guns & Roses
Goodbye My Friend – Linda Ronstadt
Can't Fell My Face – The Weeknd
It's Not Over Yet – For King & Country
Tennessee Whiskey – Chris Stapleton
Good News – Manic Drive
Boot Scootin' Boogie – Brand New Man
Keep Your Head Up – Andy Grammer
White Dress – Parachute
Wherever You Will Go – The Calling
At Last – Etta James

Printed in Great Britain
by Amazon

84736226R00120